NO EASY ANSWERS

NO EASY ANSWERS

Deanna Lueder

Women's Press
Toronto

No Easy Answers
Deanna Lueder

First published in 2008 by
Women's Press, an imprint of Canadian Scholars' Press Inc.
180 Bloor Street West, Suite 801
Toronto, Ontario
M5S 2V6

www.womenspress.ca

Canadian Scholars' Press Inc./Women's Press gratefully acknowledges financial support for our publishing activities from the Ontario Arts Council, the Canada Council for the Arts, the Government of Canada through the Book Publishing Industry Development Program (BPIDP), and the Government of Ontario through the Ontario Book Publishing Tax Credit Program.

Library and Archives Canada Cataloguing in Publication

Lueder, Deanna, 1944–
    No easy answers / Deanna Lueder.

ISBN 978-0-88961-465-9

    1. Social workers—Fiction. 2. Child welfare—Fiction. 3. Social service—Fiction. I. Title.

PS8623.U325N6 2008   C813'.6   C2008-900509-0

Book design: Em Dash Design

08   09   10   11   12   5   4   3   2   1

Printed and bound in Canada by Marquis Book Printing Inc.

To my dear family, across Canada and in Singapore, my fellow social workers, and all the brave children

CONTENTS

GROWING PAINS

WHEN HER SIX-YEAR-OLD SISTER BECAME SICK, AND THEN sicker, Lexie Doucette was four and did not fully understand what was happening. But as Peggy's moans increased, her parents grew more distracted. Finally, with rushing steps and frightened voices, they wrapped Peggy in blankets and drove off to the hospital in Winnipeg more than twenty miles away, leaving the screen door slamming behind them. They were gone all day and perhaps all night. Lexie didn't see them again until the next morning.

She and her sister Maureen were left alone to wander separately through the house, which seemed suddenly enormous and silent. Maureen, eight, had long, brown hair in braids, brown eyes, and a soft voice. She rested in the corner of the couch and wiped at the tears on her cheeks with the ribbons that tied the ends of her braids. Eventually she heated some soup their mother had left out for lunch. She cautioned Lexie to blow on each spoonful, then left her at the kitchen table. She carried her own soup and another bowl upstairs to the bedroom where ten-year-old Jeannie lay sick with a milder polio virus—the same one that had struck Maureen and Lexie two weeks earlier.

No one came near the house all that day for fear of infection, and the girls had been warned to stay indoors. Lexie gazed out the kitchen window to look longingly past her yard and the row of houses across the alley to the vast prairie beyond, interrupted only by a bluff of poplar trees surrounding a small slough. Lexie remembered nothing else of those long hours, although Maureen must have come downstairs, made some supper, and sent her to bed.

After that day, their parents took turns staying with Peggy at the hospital. Lexie remembered only a fragment of those first days, their mother at the kitchen sink washing dishes, silently wiping them dry as she watched out the window. When at last Lexie's father came up the back path that ran through the vegetable garden, Mother dropped her tea towel on the counter and hurried outside, stopping to close the screen door carefully behind her.

"Run and play, dear. Daddy and I need to talk," she instructed. But Lexie stood at the door watching, pushing her finger through a little hole in the screen, round and round until the mesh ripped. She jammed her hands into her pockets. A few yards from the door, her parents stopped and faced each other. Her mother reached up and touched her father on the shoulder. She asked him something. Lexie couldn't hear what it was, but her dad was crying. She turned away before they could see her and ran upstairs to her room, where she lay face down on the bed she normally shared with Peggy, her doll digging into her chest. If her father and mother could cry, then what was she to do? She stayed on her bed for a long time, until she heard Maureen come home.

"How's Peggy?" Maureen asked their mother, even before the front door had shut behind her.

"They've put her in an iron lung. We don't know for how long. We just have to wait."

Their father's deep voice interrupted Mother. He sounded furious and—there it was again—that frightened tone.

"I could hear her, Maureen, over all the others. I was walking up the steps to the hospital door, and I could hear her screaming. The pain, the pain when it moves into her joints."

"Shhh, don't talk about that," hushed Mother. She turned to the girls and explained, "They have all the polio victims in a separate ward near the front door. It's a hot day, so I guess the windows were open." They fell silent, and soon Father turned on the radio. When the news came on, Lexie went outside to wander around the yard. Eventually Mother called her to come and help Maureen set the table for supper. As soon as the food was set out, Mother left for the hospital.

Weeks later, when the virus had run its terrible course and Peggy had survived, their parents explained that she would have to stay in hospital many months, undergoing rehabilitation. Lexie had no idea what that meant and never asked, though she was greatly relieved that her parents were laughing together again. The house was no longer filled with overwhelming tension, and her father once again teased her and pulled her up on his lap.

Mother sewed doll's clothes for Peggy and sent batches of cookies, iced pink, and chocolate fudge, by mail. Maureen helped, her voice quiet and eager, stitching hems and embroidering little flowers on the dresses, while Jeannie stirred the fudge until it was brown and glossy in the pot. Mother gave Lexie bits of material—red taffeta, white dotted Swiss cotton—so she could make her own doll's clothes, but she was still awkward with a needle and thread, and when her stitches ravelled and her seams broke, she threw it all in the garbage in a fury. Her mother clucked her tongue, told her to take her time, to work more carefully.

"Here, Lexie, I'll help you," offered Maureen.

"Never mind. It won't turn out right anyway." Lexie sulked and stomped out to the front porch, where her mother found her a few minutes later.

"I've fixed a plate of cookies and fudge for you and Isabella." Mother handed her a dish. "Isabella likes fudge, doesn't she?"

"She's just a doll," Lexie fumed. "You know she can't eat food."

• ◆ •

When Peggy finally came home nearly a year later, clad in blankets and the antiseptic, sterile smell of the hospital, Lexie hardly knew what to say to her.

"Hi, Peggy." She glanced uncertainly at her mother. "I'm glad you're home."

"Hi," whispered Peggy. Then she was silent as Mother fussed over her blanket. She lay exactly as Dad had placed her, without movement, except for the moment when she had raised her head slightly to peer at Lexie. Then she rested without speaking for a long time.

Lexie ran upstairs and picked up Isabella from her bed. She carried her downstairs and offered her to Peggy. "I guess your doll's still packed. Here, you can hold Isabella." Peggy glanced briefly at the doll but didn't respond.

Mother whispered to Lexie, "Give her time. She hasn't seen you for eleven months." This seemed odd to Lexie. Even though she had been shy with Peggy, too, she certainly hadn't forgotten her. But for all she knew, this could be what happened to people in hospitals, one of those things people expected her to know.

The polio had left Peggy's back stooped, her fingers bony and bent, her legs thin and white with great knobbly knees, and her feet twisted. Only her thick, curly dark hair, great green eyes, and open mouth with the spittle running down—a sign of brain damage at birth—were unchanged.

Their parents bought Peggy a new tricycle, big and orange and white. Her father made special blocks that he attached to the pedals. They bought her a new doll carriage, blue and cream coloured, and they weighted the bottom, under the mattress, with heavy books so that she could lean on it for balance as she pushed it along. They told Lexie that Peggy needed these new things so she could learn to walk again. It seemed clear to Lexie that she could make better use of them than Peggy, who had to be helped to stand, let alone ride a tricycle or push a carriage. But she knew better than to express this sentiment, and she understood implicitly that there wasn't enough money for new toys for her as well as the items Peggy required.

As Peggy began the slow process of learning to walk again, she often fell heavily to the ground, crashing down on the cement sidewalk and then crying helplessly, unable to get up. Each time her knees bled anew, opening up the scabs from the previous day's efforts. Lexie couldn't understand why Peggy never seemed to learn how to protect herself, and she would shout, furious with frustration, "Put your hands out. Put your hands out when you fall!" But Peggy never seemed to remember. She was so thin and brittle that when she lost her balance and collapsed, Lexie held her breath, afraid that she would break. Lexie learned to get down on her hands and knees when Peggy fell. Then Peggy would put her arms around Lexie's neck and cling against her back, and as Lexie slowly stood, Peggy rose as well.

Mother made bandages every day from old sheets and flour or sugar bags, long white strips wound round and round Peggy's swollen knees to cover the great gashes and crusted blood thickly glazed over with Dr. Watkins Salve. Every morning that summer, with her knees in the bandages that gradually drooped, became soiled, and ravelled, Peggy carefully lifted each stiff leg with her twisted, misshapen hands until her feet rested on the pedals of her tricycle. She would strain to push the pedals around and move slowly down the sidewalk.

One day when he was visiting Peggy, the family doctor brought over a tricycle for Lexie. It was an old one that had belonged to his daughter, and he had accidentally driven over it. Lexie's dad pounded it back into shape.

"There," he said. "Paint's a bit chipped, but she's as good as new." Lexie hated it.

In the afternoons while Peggy slept, Lexie threw aside her old second-hand tricycle and took Peggy's, pedalling madly and singing out loud. The lawns blurred as she rushed by. Once, she took the books out of the carriage and flung them onto the front porch, along with Peggy's doll. She put Isabella carefully into the carriage and pushed it to her friend Wendy's house. But all too soon, Mother called her home to play with Peggy. "Oh, do I have to? I always have to play with her!" She huffed her shoulders and whined, "She's so slow. It's so boring!"

Lexie stomped her feet and scowled as fiercely as she dared, but eventually she forgot her anger. Peggy waited silently as always, seemingly unfazed by Lexie's outburst, and then played "French" with her. In the game, Lexie, who couldn't speak French, would imitate their aunties and their father in total gibberish full of the rises, falls, and inflections that she had heard. Peggy would laugh with delight and respond in turn.

❧

One day the Indians came to town, as they did every summer, several wagons full of families, each pulled by a team of horses. They set up their tents on the edge of town, at the end of Lexie's street. All the neighbourhood children were under strict instructions to stay away from them. The Indian women came door to door, asking for food or old clothes. Lexie's mother gave them vegetables from the garden, fresh bread, and the old clothes she had collected over the past year, the same clothes that Lexie had been using to play dress-up. When she complained bitterly after they left, her mother glared at her. "They need those clothes and you don't. Now quit pouting and run and play."

Peggy and Lexie sat on the front steps and watched the wagons go by, the horses slowly clip-clopping to the big pasture at the end of the street. The children in the crowded wagons stared back silently at the two girls. A woman suddenly jumped off the edge of one wagon and hurried toward them, pulling something from her shirt pocket. She pressed it into Peggy's hand and said, "For you, crippled girl." Peggy and Lexie watched open-mouthed as she ran back to the wagon still moving down the street. Peggy opened her hand to show Lexie what she held. It was a dollar bill, folded in tiny squares, soft with age. Neither child had ever had paper money before, only pennies and nickels. Lexie called to their mother, "Mom, come and see! Come and see quick what the Indians gave to Peggy!" But Peggy cried, "She called me a crippled girl. How could she tell that? I was just sitting here. I wasn't walking or anything."

Lexie looked at her sister carefully while Mother comforted her. Her shoulders were bony and white against her halter top. Her legs, bandaged and twisted, were so thin that her shorts gaped around her thighs. Her face was pale with big eyes full of tears, and her mouth was hanging open with spittle running down, unchecked in her distress. Then Lexie began to cry, too, but she could not have said why.

○ ◆ ○

That fall Peggy and Lexie began grade one together. Jeannie, having skipped grade three years ago, had begun secondary school already, located in another direction. So it was Maureen's job to pull Peggy to and from school in the wagon. But at school, they hardly saw Maureen. She became foreign, one of the big girls who sat on the wide cement steps at the front door, and who whispered and giggled and pushed one another. The younger children wandered about, skipped rope, played marbles. Lexie was never sure what to do with herself. Peggy stayed in at recess to rest, although sometimes in good weather she came outside to lean against the railing, silently watching the other children.

When winter set in on the flat prairie, with its freezing wind and drifting pebbles of icy snow, the mornings were dark when they left for school, and it was dark again as they came home. With her brown braids hanging down from her yellow wool cap and falling against her coat, Maureen pulled Peggy, who sat motionless on a sled, wrapped in blankets. Lexie danced around them in her red snowsuit.

When it was bitterly cold, twenty degrees below zero or more, they wore toques and wound scarves around their foreheads and cheeks and over their noses and mouths, until only their eyes showed. Their eyelashes and nostril hairs would frost up; it was a peculiar sensation. Then Lexie would move closer to Maureen, sometimes helping her pull the sled rope, until her hands grew numb with the cold, even through two pairs of mittens. They travelled down the frozen gravel road from the white stucco school, past the thin bluff of black willows with the pale prairie opening beyond, past the co-op store, past the corner where the three black Labrador dogs habitually barked and circled them, round the corner to where the wind waited, past the vacant lot to their house.

Their mother watched for them every day, holding their new baby sister to the window of the living room. Maureen and Lexie would wave at their mother. Maureen always remembered an extra wave for Giselle, but Lexie never did. In her view, this pretty blonde-haired baby was a nuisance, taking even more of her parents' attention. By then Peggy was so stiff and cold that both Maureen and Lexie had to help her off the sled and drag her into the house. Mother would check her hands and feet for frostbite. On the coldest days, despite Peggy's protests, Mother kept her home.

Sometimes Peggy's legs ached so badly at the end of the day that she cried as she lay on the couch. Then their mother made hot compresses and took turns with their father wrapping them around her legs. Lexie watched from her secret cave under the dining room table, hidden by the long cloth. She tried to imagine Peggy's pain, stretching her own firm legs in front of her.

At the end of June, when all the children raced out of the school, whooping with their report cards in their hands, Peggy walked slowly with her sisters' help, carrying only a note, carefully folded in an envelope. Lexie's body teemed with joy at the praise and promotion her report card contained. But she also felt a stab of compassion for Peggy and, in equal measure, a stab of anger at their teacher. Why couldn't she have given Peggy a report card like everyone else's, never mind what was in it?

In July Peggy went back to the hospital for an operation. At bedtime one night after she had gone, Mother explained.

"It's called a spinal fusion. It will help straighten her back. The doctors say if she doesn't have the operation, her back will get more and more crooked. She'll be gone about six weeks, and then she'll have to wear a cast for a year."

"How big a cast?" Lexie asked.

"From her neck to here." She pointed to the bottom of Lexie's spine.

Lexie's throat tightened, and she could hardly speak. "Won't it hurt? Won't she be lonesome?"

Her mother pulled the blanket up to Lexie's chin and brushed the hair back off her forehead. "She'll be all right. Daddy and I will visit her every day while she's in the hospital. But when she comes home, she won't be able to climb the staircase for another year. She won't be able to move."

Mother kissed her good night, and as she paused by the door, Lexie asked, "Mom, can I help you sew doll's clothes this time?"

Her mother turned. "Why, yes. You're big enough now to reach the treadle."

"Can I make some doll's clothes for me, too? Will you help me do the sewing?" Lexie imagined an elegant blue velvet coat for her doll.

"Yes. We'll do it together." Mother switched off the light, and Lexie heard her slowly walking down the stairs.

When they had made Peggy's doll's clothes, Lexie's mother helped her cut out and sew a blue coat. She also sewed a delicate dress of pale rose satin. Lexie proudly dressed Isabella in her wonderful new clothes and laid her in Peggy's empty carriage.

But as she pushed it down the street, she imagined Peggy leaning against the carriage, laboriously pushing it along the sidewalk. Soon she returned home and took her doll back into the kitchen, where her mother was packing Peggy's parcel.

As if Lexie had known all along what she would do, she took the coat and dress off Isabella. They had given her no pleasure except in the making. "Here, Mom. Pack these for Peggy." She ran out of the kitchen up to her room, lonely without Peggy, and lay on her bed, staring at the ceiling.

LEAVING HOME

WHEN LEXIE'S MOTHER TOOK LEXIE TO SCHOOL THAT FIRST morning, she went confidently, sure of her place in the world. She was prepared for the rows of desks, for the blackboard and wall maps and readers, and she had also been prepared for a teacher to whom everyone deferred. Nevertheless, she suddenly felt sick and small, and would not let her mother leave the room, even though Miss Walker pointed out that all the other parents had long since gone home. Too frightened of the teacher to protest further, Lexie finally watched her mother leave the classroom apologetically.

Alien smells—chalk dust, old rubber boots and sweaty socks, crisp new paper and mimeograph ink—mingled with Miss Walker's perfume and face powder as she bent over Lexie's desk, watching her carefully print her name. Lexie retreated from the huge face that loomed over her, as far as her desk allowed. She nodded mutely when the teacher remarked that she had taught Lexie's older sisters and that they had been excellent students. It seemed clear to Lexie that Miss Walker did not think she would ever be as good as her sisters. She felt sure that the teacher had looked her up and down with great disdain before moving on to the next student.

For the rest of the first week—Peggy wouldn't start till the next Monday so the teacher could give her more attention—Lexie went to school with her older sister Maureen, who ceased to acknowledge her as soon as they arrived, and left her at the "baby" side of the yard. There, Lexie wandered until the bell rang, then lined up with the other first graders.

That Saturday, Lexie hurried through her after-supper chores—carrying the dishes from the dining room to the kitchen and drying them after her older sisters took turns washing—so that she could be the first one to see the Saturday edition of the comics in the newspaper. She had long envied the casual way in which her sisters decoded the words in the clouds over the cartoon characters' heads and was now triumphantly ready to read them herself. But the miracle did not happen. Though she could recognize all the letters, she still could not form more than three or four of them into words. The stories remained largely a mystery to her. She knew then that she had been betrayed. They had all lied to her. Everyone had said she would learn to read in school. Now here she had attended a full, hateful week and still could not read.

In disgust, she threw the comic section onto the floor and glared at her mother and father, who were seated comfortably in their respective easy chairs, each reading a section of the newspaper. They were oblivious to her. "That's it!" Lexie declared. "I'm not going to school any more because that stupid teacher never taught me to read."

Her father rustled his newspaper and kept reading. Her mother lowered her paper long enough to frown and say, "Don't call your teacher stupid. Nobody learns to read in the first week of school."

Jeannie and Maureen, who had come into the living room in time to hear the exchange, tittered. Lexie was enraged. She scowled at her sisters and stomped her feet. "Nobody's helping me." Still holding her section of the paper, Lexie's mother explained something about phonics and practice. But Lexie had made up her mind. Her mother finally became impatient and declared, "For heaven's sake, wipe that scowl off your face. You're going to school, and that's final."

Lexie knew she had lost the battle; her mother would not relent. "Okay. I'll go," she agreed sullenly. Then she stomped from the room, shouting as mutinously as she dared, "But I'll hate every minute of it!" As she heard Jeannie and Maureen still laughing in the background, a part of her knew she was being absurd. She slammed her bedroom door, knowing that her mother would allow her this one expression of frustration, of powerlessness, to make up for her sisters' cruelty.

She returned to school Monday morning and, sighing deeply, stood at the entrance. In grade one, the children did not form a clique so much as a shifting, formless amoeba, bumping together and apart in confusion about this new world of incomprehensible rules and expectations. But gradually Lexie made a few friends.

There was Astrid Ericksson, whose skin and hair were the whitest Lexie had ever seen. Astrid chewed her fingernails to the quick. The habit fascinated Lexie, who tried it herself but stopped after one effort, mystified by Astrid's addiction.

Then there was Vera Dombrowsky, a round and red-cheeked girl with short, curly, taffy-coloured hair. She lived on a farm and rode the school bus every day, an experience that Lexie and the other town children envied.

But the best of the friends Lexie made was Maude Carney, her light brown hair cut so short that she was teased for looking like a boy. She wore glasses and stuttered. Maude lived alone with her mother in a room over the Blue Bird Café, opposite the school. Her mother worked there as a waitress. Lexie had never before known anyone who lived like this, whose mother went off to work every day. Maude was left to wash and dress herself, and she ate all her meals in a booth down below in the café. It seemed very glamorous.

In response to the other children's questions, Maude told stories about letters and presents she received from her father. She variously said that he lived in Montreal or Toronto or New York—huge cities thousands of miles from their small town. No one really believed the stories; several children scoffed at them and teased Maude whenever she stuttered. But Vera, Astrid, and Lexie stood up for her until everyone else grew bored with the teasing and wandered away.

In October, after a birthday party at Astrid's house, Lexie came home and placed her basket of party favours on the coffee table, asking her mother to keep the baby away. The basket contained candy, a tiny pleated parasol, and a miniature plastic doll, naked except for a scrap of diaper. Breathlessly, Lexie described Astrid's house, "—and she has her own bedroom. All to herself. She has no brothers or sisters. Her bed has a cloth roof over it."

"That's a canopy," interrupted her mother.

"Yeah. And she has her own dollhouse, just like the one at school. And a million books and puzzles and games."

"Hmmm…." Lexie's mother sighed.

Lexie spied her baby sister's chubby hands clasped tightly around the tiny doll, the basket tipped on the floor. "Gee, Astrid and Maude are so lucky." She pulled the broken doll from Giselle and stooped to gather the contents of the basket. "No sisters or brothers. Boy, it must be great!"

"Wait and see, Lexie. You'll be glad you have sisters someday," her mother counselled as she picked up the crying Giselle and soothed her with kisses. But the wealth of Astrid's belongings—far more toys than Lexie and all her sisters had together—and the cosy room Maude shared with her mother—and only her mother—seemed far superior to Lexie's existence with four sisters, two of whom she was expected to share and play with and two more who bossed her around, or worse yet, ignored her.

Lexie learned to read before Halloween, but her mother made her continue on in school anyway, pointing out that she still had to master arithmetic.

The grade one class was dismissed each day at three-thirty, while the other classes continued until four o'clock. Vera had to wait for the school bus to come. Maureen didn't get out of class for another thirty minutes, and Peggy always spent this time resting on a cot in the school nurse's office. Soon Lexie and Vera began going to Maude's for that half hour. Each day, as they passed through the café to the inner staircase leading upstairs, Maude's mother winked and gave them each a donut.

In Lexie's estimation, Mrs. Carney was beautiful. With her long, curly black hair, thick makeup, and scarlet lips, she did not look like a mother at all. She was thin in her pale blue uniform, and she wore matching blue rhinestone earrings that hung to her shoulders. She always seemed happy to see them and never scolded or corrected Maude in the way of other mothers.

Their single room, which Maude referred to as an apartment, was long and narrow. The kitchen area contained a small refrigerator and a hot plate, which sat on a counter next to the sink. A short clothesline had been strung above the sink, from which several of

Mrs. Carney's lacy bras and panties always hung to dry. A chrome table with two chairs was pushed below the only window in the room, and the couch at the far end, Maude explained, opened out to a bed, where she and her mother slept. They shared a bathroom with several other tenants. Lexie thought it seemed quite comfy compared to her own tall three-storey house.

"What do you do when we're not here and your mom's working?" asked Vera.

"I play with my doll or s-s-sit downstairs and watch."

"Wow, can you eat whatever you want?"

"P-p-pretty much. But on S-Saturdays, I go to my Auntie Joan's and stay overnight."

"Overnight?"

"Yeah. S-s-so Mom can go out. S-sometimes she has a boyfriend. Then she p-picks me up on S-Sunday afternoon. That's her day off."

"Why's your hair so short?"

Maude ducked her head, embarrassed. "I got lice at my other s-s-school and Auntie Joan cut it all off. My mom was real mad—at Auntie Joan, n-not me. I used to have long hair."

"You went to another school? You mean you failed?" Vera was astonished.

"I did not fail! I was in Kindergarten. You don't even have Kindergarten in this hick town." She pushed her glasses back up the bridge of her nose. "*Hick town.* That's what my mom calls this p-p-place." Vera and Lexie fell silent, absorbing this information. *What was* lice*? What did* hick *mean? What was it like having a mom who had boyfriends?*

One day, Vera invited Maude and Lexie to ride the school bus to her farm home the next afternoon. If their mothers allowed them, she explained, her dad would drive the girls home before supper, as soon as he finished milking. They hopped on the bus after school the next day.

Vera lived in a new house all on one floor. Her mother silently opened the back door and watched closely while they removed their winter boots. She hung up their snowsuits as they followed Vera into the kitchen. Vera showed them her new baby sister, sleeping in a carriage. On the floor near the table, her two younger brothers played quietly with toy trucks.

Everything was shiny and clean and silent, except for the humming of the refrigerator. Vera took Lexie and Maude down a long hallway to her bedroom. There were no carpets anywhere, apart from a carefully aligned rug beside her bed. Other than the bed and the baby's crib, the only piece of furniture was a chest of drawers. Vera had a few toys stored under her bed, and they examined them politely. Instinctively, they kept their voices lowered, until Vera's mother called, "Vera, come out of there."

"We're coming," Vera answered, immediately taking the toys from the girls' hands and pushing them back under the bed.

Mrs. Dombrowsky had prepared a snack for them, and they sat at the kitchen table to eat it. The little brothers moved their game to a corner of the room, still playing silently. It seemed curious to Lexie that they didn't clamour to sit at the table and have some of the oatmeal raisin cookies, washed down with homemade root beer. That is certainly what would have happened at her house. Except for the root beer. Her mother did not make such a drink. Lexie had never tasted anything so delicious, and she and Maude quickly emptied their glasses. "Boy, that was good," Lexie exclaimed hopefully.

"Would you like more? I'll ask Mom." Vera slid off her chair purposefully and hurried across the room to her mother, who was kneading dough. "Mom, Maude and Lexie would like more root beer."

Without a word, Vera's mother turned and slapped her across the face. The sound rang out in the room. The boys continued their silent play, never looking up. Vera returned to the table without crying. The cookie Lexie had been eating turned dry in her mouth, and Maude was trembling. They sat wordlessly, chewing ashes, pretending not to notice the large red welt on Vera's cheek or the tears that were beginning to seep down.

Lexie wanted to go home, but she remembered that they had to wait for Vera's dad to finish milking. "Let's go outside," she whispered. They pushed back their chairs and quickly dressed in the hallway. "Thank you, Mrs. Dombrowsky," quavered Lexie. Maude stuttered her thanks, already half out the door. Vera's mother nodded, never turning away from her dough. The boys glanced up without expression.

The girls never referred to their visit to Vera's house again, and Lexie told no one about the experience. But every night for weeks, after her mother turned off the bedroom light, she saw and heard that hard smack on Vera's cheek. Maude came to Lexie's house after school two or three times, but Vera was not allowed to go because she would miss her school bus. Even when Lexie's dad offered to drive her home, permission was not given. So they resumed their daily treks to Maude's apartment. But when they returned to school after the Christmas holiday, Maude told them that her mother was in the hospital and she had to live with Auntie Joan for a few days.

These days stretched into weeks, and although Maude's hair grew longer and her aunt made her new dresses with matching bows for her hair, Maude herself seemed to be shrinking. Her stuttering grew worse, and she rarely spoke to anyone except Vera and Lexie. Sister Mary Josephine, the school principal, came to their classroom one day and asked that they say a prayer every morning for Maude's mother, who was gravely ill. Lexie prayed fervently.

After school one late winter afternoon, Maude declared that she was going to the hospital to see her mother and asked Lexie if she would like to come. This was the first time Maude had spoken that day. Lexie was so glad to hear her voice that she agreed, even though she suspected that children weren't allowed into hospitals alone. They walked hand in hand down the long blocks to the centre of town, where the large, red brick hospital loomed at the end of Main Street. The nurses knew Maude and asked her where her aunt was.

"S-s-she's coming. We ran ahead."

They were allowed to enter the room where Maude's mother lay. The bed was so high, they could hardly see her until they climbed onto the visitor's chair that they had pulled next to it. Lexie barely recognized Mrs. Carney. Her luxurious black hair lay limp and damp on the pillow around her white face. Her lips, without the wonderful red, red lipstick, were pale and bluish. Her eyes fluttered open and shut. Tubes and needles were stuck into her long, thin arms. But when Maude kissed her and took her hand, she wet her lips and smiled.

"Lexie's here, too, Mom."

Her mother nodded slightly.

Then a nurse entered the room and sent the girls out. "We've phoned your aunt. She didn't know you'd come! You shouldn't be here without her," she scolded. "Your mother needs her rest. Hurry home now."

Maude's aunt lived halfway between the hospital and the school, and she was waiting for them at her front gate. "You come in, too, Lexie. I've phoned your mother, and your sister is coming to get you. You girls had us worried. We didn't know where you were."

But Lexie's mother didn't scold her when Maureen brought her home. Nor did her father when he came home from work and heard the whole story, although both parents pointed out that it wasn't to happen again.

Maude was missing from school for several weeks after that. Sister Mary Josephine came into the classroom one morning to make an announcement: Maude Carney's mother had died. In the hush that followed this news, she softly continued that though they knew Maude would miss her mother, they must not be too sad. Maude would be well cared for by her aunt. "Now," Sister Mary Josephine went on, "We must pray for Mrs. Carney's soul so that she can join our Lord in heaven." Lexie stood with the other students and knelt obediently by her desk.

But she prayed, not for Mrs. Carney to reach heaven, but for a miracle for Maude to make her mother wake up and return to their apartment over the Blue Bird Café. She had, however, no real faith that this would happen.

It wasn't until after Easter that Maude finally returned to school. Lexie stood beside her at recess, and after a few uneasy moments, she asked her if she would like to play marbles. They crouched down. Lexie shared out her marbles as Maude picked up a stick and began to dig a small hole in which to shoot them. She stopped suddenly and tossed the stick aside.

"Did you know that my mother died?" Lexie nodded and Maude continued. "Yes. She did. They dug a hole six feet deep and stuck her down there in a box." She glared furiously out across the playground.

Lexie did not know what to say. She didn't know why Maude was so angry, so outraged, that her words came out without a false start, without a stutter. Lexie could have understood if Maude had cried. Then she could have put her arms around her to comfort her the way her mother comforted Giselle, but what was she to do with anger? She bent her head and shot her first marble. She picked her best shooter, and through a throat painfully thickened, she said, "It's your turn, Maude."

SALVATION

IN 1958, WHEN TWELVE-YEAR-OLD LEXIE WAS ASKED WHAT she wanted for Christmas, she modestly suggested, "Oh, nothing much. Maybe some panties or a new rosary." Her sisters shrugged at each other and walked away. This new Lexie with her passionate Catholicism was puzzling and annoying. Her mother pursed her lips and rolled her eyes. She muttered, "And this too shall pass," continuing with her housework. And though this hostility hurt a bit, Lexie persevered, following the path of martyrs before her, sure that her deep sense of what was right would save them all.

She was prepared. She was grimly determined to put the real meaning of Christmas back into their lives. She had glared at her father when he brought home wine and whiskey for the season and had not spoken to him for several days, although she wasn't sure that he even noticed. She imagined dramatically splashing the liquor down the sink, her father thanking her profusely for saving him from sin. She didn't dare do it, though.

Everyone around her seemed to be heading for damnation, or at least years in purgatory: Giselle, with her enormous Christmas list, complete with catalogue numbers and prices carefully printed by each item; Jeannie and Maureen and Peggy, with their lists of cosmetics, clothes, and jewellery; and her mother rushing about, cranky and impatient. Her father was oblivious to it all.

Lexie was going through a pudgy stage. She had just been prescribed eyeglasses and was discovering the ongoing misery of adolescent acne. "Plain as a mud fence," she told herself in front of the mirror and decided there was nothing to be done for it. She would enter a convent, the one place she could think of where outward looks didn't matter. She was attending a parochial school, where she had embraced Catholicism with a fervour that irritated her mother, a reluctant Catholic by marriage, and confounded her father, a nominal Catholic except at Easter and Christmas.

Like most of her friends' fathers, Lexie's dad was out of the house all day, working as an auto mechanic. Her mother, who toiled endlessly in the home caring for them all, never failed to heave a sigh of relief and light a cigarette at the end of each day, when supper was over and the kitchen was spotless again. Each time Lexie caught her mother smoking, she surreptitiously crossed herself and sent upward a brief, silent prayer for her. But she had to be careful—her mother became really annoyed if she caught Lexie at it.

One evening, Lexie's mother allowed herself an extra cigarette and then announced to her daughters, who were starting school holidays the next day, "Tomorrow we'll begin a major cleaning of the entire house. So don't be making any plans for the next three or four mornings, girls. I expect you up by eight-thirty, and if you get your jobs done, you can be entirely free for the afternoons."

The next morning, after a quick breakfast, the sisters began their tasks, although the odd squabble broke out. Mother issued orders and reprimands from the kitchen, where wonderful smells of Christmas baking were beginning to waft. "Lexie, quit pestering Jeannie and get back to washing those stairs, and mind you get the railings while you're at it."

"But Mom, she walked on them when they were still wet!"

"How else am I s'posed to get upstairs?" shouted Jeannie.

"Just get on with it." Mother slammed the oven door shut and called to Maureen. "When you're finished in the bathroom, don't forget to change the bedding in the spare room. Peggy can help you. Giselle, be sure to polish every key on that piano. They're all sticky." Then her voice subsided. "Damn kids. How many times do I have to tell them to wash their hands before they practise?"

Auntie Mary, Uncle Frank, and their four daughters were driving down for Christmas from Selkirk, a small city about eighty miles northwest of Grand Coulee. Auntie Mary was Lexie's mother's sister, and Lexie's father was much less enthusiastic about the plan than the rest of the family. He and Uncle Frank were known to disagree on everything from the colour of the sky to the Liberal Party of Canada. Lexie and her sisters, however, were very fond of Uncle Frank, who had the gift of noticing them as individuals rather than as a single unit known as "Margaret and Gilles's girls."

Lexie's mother chatted quietly to Auntie Mary over the phone just days before Christmas. Lexie overheard her mother in the kitchen that evening, speaking to her father. "Gilles, Mary and I have been talking. When Frank comes, you must get along with him—at least tolerate him for the few days he'll be here. Mary will ask the same of Frank, so I don't see why you both can't act like reasonable adults for three days." There was no response from Lexie's dad, other than the sound of his newspaper as he snapped it open.

The girls' housework finally met with their mother's approval. The baking was done, the last gingerbread was iced, the tourtière was made, and the huge turkey sat thawing in the refrigerator, complacently awaiting its big day.

Lexie's dad brought in the Christmas tree and amid wildly conflicting advice, set it up. He attached all the strings of lights, lost his temper, sorted them out, and lost it again as he attempted to discover which light was causing the whole string to black out. This was standard Christmas procedure. Lexie and her sisters pulled out the boxes of decorations as he cursed and occasionally brandished his fist at the lights. At one point, he became so outraged that he shook the tree as if he were throttling it. From time to time, one or another of the girls offered advice until he began to look at them desperately and—could it be?—with regret that he had fathered all of them. In the nick of time, their mother brought in cocoa and the first taste of the Christmas baking.

Their father sat back then, his work done. A glass of wine magically appeared in his hand. Lexie gritted her teeth and shook her head. He ignored her.

The girls trimmed the tree with the same decorations every year. Each object elicited a squeal of recollection from one of them. Jeannie began to sing carols, and everyone joined in. Their father always sang "Ave Maria" and a French-Canadian carol that began "Il est née le divin enfant." It had a beautiful melody, and the others, unable to speak the French that was Father's first language, hummed and stuttered along.

The relatives arrived the next evening, nearly frozen because the car heater was defective and it was thirty degrees below zero outside. As they placed their presents under the tree, greed began to grow in Lexie's heart and in the hearts of her sisters and cousins. The nine girls indulged in a frenzy of pawing through the presents, reading the labels, and shaking and squeezing, until their mother and Auntie Mary came in from the kitchen and proclaimed the law of "no touching."

Lexie was deeply ashamed at how easily her resolve had been broken in the excitement of the moment. She withdrew to the couch and watched as the other girls giggled and chattered. They talked of boyfriends, parties, clothes, and hairstyles. A contemptuous sneer twisted her lips as they went on and on with their frivolous prattle, and she resolved again to be a better person. Tomorrow she would go to early Mass, never mind how cold and dark it would be. They would all be sleeping while she was praying for them.

When Lexie returned from church the next morning, everyone had finished breakfast and no one seemed to have noticed her sacrifice. The older girls were two and three at a time in the bathroom, fighting over mirror space and moaning with anguish over minute flaws. Lexie tried to ignore the endless discussions over nail polish, hairspray, eye shadow, lip gloss versus lipstick, and whether it would be too much to apply a beauty spot like Elizabeth Taylor's. Giselle and her matching cousin were having a wonderful time spying on the girls and running like mad when spotted. Lexie glowered at them all. Where was the true spirit of Christmas?

Christmas Eve dinner was a French-Canadian meal in the Doucette household, and this year they were having tourtière. Uncle Frank, of Irish-American Protestant heritage, launched into a lecture on the origin of the dish and French-Canadian culture in general. He was a genuine scholar with an intense desire to share what he had learned in his research, but it wasn't always appreciated.

Lexie's father began to glare and the table grew quiet—but Uncle Frank continued on, blithely unaware of the building tension. Lexie's mother and Auntie Mary began a loud discussion amid much passing of food, hoping to drown out his voice. Giselle saved the situation quite accidentally by spilling her milk all over Uncle Frank's lap. In all the upheaval, he lost the thread of his dissertation and everyone relaxed. As a sort of silent reward, dad took Giselle on his knee, where she remained until dessert.

Even Lexie was happy with the rest of Christmas Eve, although in deference to their Protestant relatives, the Doucettes didn't attend midnight Mass. But the sounds of sweet carols, affectionate laughter, and a sense of delightful anticipation soothed Lexie. As she squinted at the tree lights to make them blur, she piously thanked God for anything she might get the next morning. Once again, she reminded Him that despite the wine her parents were sipping, they weren't actually bad people. And although she feared her shallow sisters were hopeless, she prayed for them, too.

For the family and their visitors, Christmas morning dawned long before the sun came up. They opened their presents. The other girls whooped over new crinolines, coloured tights, felt skirts embossed with poodles or guitars or pianos, sweater sets, cosmetics, bracelets, and earrings. Lexie got thirteen sets of panties in every colour of the rainbow, and some were even embroidered with days of the week. She also got four rosaries. She politely thanked everyone.

After her breakfast, which tasted unaccountably dry, Lexie retreated to her room with her piles of panty sets, the rosaries sacrilegiously slung over her arm. Even up there, she could hear the squeals of laughter two storeys below. Suddenly her door was thrown open, and Jeannie walked in. She was a lot like their mother: brisk, and crisp and tart like apples in the fall. She held out a pair of new black tights. Mother had told Lexie she was too young for black anything, but Jeannie wore nothing else. She was majoring in fine arts at university and considered herself a bohemian.

"Here," she said. "I'll trade you these for one set of panties."

"Will they fit?" Lexie temporized. Then, thinking of God, she resisted a nearly overwhelming urge to grab the tights from her sister's hand.

"Sure, they're one-size-fits-all." She poked through Lexie's panty pile and picked out a set. "These will fit me. How about it?"

"Well, okay." Lexie fought for restraint and added gruffly, "If you're sure you want to." Jeannie grinned, nodded her head, and gave her sister a quick hug. Tears swelled up in Lexie's eyes as Jeannie handed her the tights.

A few minutes later, the door thumped open and in flounced the sunny, blonde Giselle, who followed Lexie everywhere. She bounced onto Lexie's bed and knocked over the remaining twelve panty sets. Peggy, fourteen now, limped more slowly into the room.

"What do you guys want?" Lexie grumbled.

"It's my room, too, you know, you know," sang Giselle.

"Lexie, are you sad?" asked Peggy anxiously.

"Heck no, why should I be?"

"We want to trade." Giselle was all business now. She pulled out a new diary from her housecoat pocket. Lexie wanted it. Shame-lessly she pawned off the panties embroidered with the days of the week.

"You'll grow into them," she urged Giselle when she held them up suspiciously.

Peggy had brought a new manicure set in a shiny red leather case for trading. Lexie offered her a rosary with blue beads and a silver cross. Satisfied with their swaps, Giselle and Peggy left to show them to Jeannie.

Their cousin Fawn rushed in shortly after. Fawn could giggle better than anyone Lexie knew, and she giggled now. "What are you going to do with all those panties? I know. Just a minute." She ran to the bedroom she was sharing with her sisters and returned a few seconds later. "I got this set of lipsticks but they're all pink. I look like death in pink. But they'd be great with your brown eyes."

"Here," Lexie said, giving up all pretense of dignity. "Let's swap. Look at the lace on these panties, a different colour on every pair. They'll fit you perfectly."

Fawn agreed and showed her how to put on lipstick and even how to take a bit on her fingertip and rub it vigorously onto her cheeks.

"You look great," she assured Lexie, before returning downstairs.

The day was getting better and better. Lexie put on her new black tights, a white blouse, and a blue skirt. She examined herself in the mirror and sighed heavily. She looked fat and boring. Then Maureen, who was sixteen, slipped in. She backcombed Lexie's hair and made spit curls around her forehead. She said she liked her lipstick, admired her tights. She lent Lexie a pale pink sweater to match the lipstick. Then she gave her a pink beaded necklace in trade for a coral rosary.

Lexie followed Maureen downstairs. Her dad hugged her and said, "There's my Christmas girl." Her mother handed her a big package. "We forgot to put this under the tree. It must have fallen to the back of my dresser." Inside was a black felt skirt with a pink poodle embossed on it. Lexie squealed and rushed back upstairs to put it on.

All the girls followed her and crowded into the bedroom. Lexie giggled as she twirled in front of the mirror. Everyone else oohed and aahed. She mentioned the name of a boy she liked. The others nodded and gave her sage advice. Then they left to get dressed themselves, calling, "Come and help, Lexie."

She nodded. She would. But first she picked up her remaining rosaries and put them in the drawer of her bedside table, along with her prayer missal.

"I'll go to Mass tomorrow," she appeased God silently.

ON BECOMING A WOMAN

A YEAR PASSED, AND CHRISTMAS WAS JUST THREE WEEKS AWAY. After evening choir rehearsal, Lexie, now thirteen, leaned back in the bus seat and daydreamed. Riding this new local service made her feel sophisticated, as if she were in a big city—especially after dark. Regular practice for the upcoming concert and High Mass usually took place between eleven-thirty and noon every Tuesday and Thursday. She had joined the school choir as soon as she had been eligible, when she turned twelve. It meant getting out of class early twice a week and, more importantly, being labelled as a senior student in the eyes of everyone at St. Mary's Elementary.

She rubbed her mitten against the frosted bus window and peered out. Then she pulled the rope to ring the bell. As the bus wheezed to a stop, she stepped out into falling snow. It drifted aimlessly downward, gradually covering the old crust of ice on the sidewalks. Lexie held her breath while the bus pulled away, white clouds of exhaust trailing behind. She began to hum as she walked home, two blocks away. Then, as no one seemed to be around, she boldly sang aloud, "Ave, Ave, Ave Marie … ee … ee … uh …" Her voice squeaked on the last note, and she giggled. She stopped and raised her face to the snow. It lightened the night from black to grey, and a white sparkling halo shone around each street lamp. The thick flakes fell over her face, on her lips, and into her open eyes. *It's so beautiful. More beautiful than the church, even. Singing at midnight Mass, everything will be white and gold.*

She reached down and scooped some fresh snow into her mitten. As she delicately touched her tongue to its tingling cold, she heard footsteps behind her. Heavy and plodding, they crunched through the snow and ice. *It's a man.* She hurried a few steps. *That's silly. Don't scare yourself.*

She slowed down again when she could see her house, now just half a block away, across the street. The front curtains were open. She could see the lights on the Christmas tree and the back of her father's head. He and Mother would be watching television.

Just as she began to hurry again, she heard the footsteps immediately behind her. Someone grasped her arms and pinned them to her sides. Lexie was paralyzed. She smelled beer, cigarette smoke, the clean scent of fresh snow melting on his jacket. She wanted to scream, but she could not make a sound. She was not able to move or call out. This astounded her. She stared toward her house, willing her father to turn around. He didn't move. The man put his head down into the back of her collar, against her neck. He was muttering something. She could feel his breath as he spoke and see the white vapour his words made, but she couldn't understand him. He lifted his head. She heard him sigh. He released her arms and gave her back a push, away from him.

Then Lexie ran. She ran into the road and down the street to her house. She raced up the front steps. Once her hand was on the doorknob, she looked back. The man had turned the other way and was briefly illuminated under a street lamp. He was short and stocky, anonymous in his dark winter clothing. The wind caught him as he turned down the side street, and he hunched against it, staggering slightly. *Drunk … he must be drunk.*

As she opened the front door, she glanced to the living room. The sliding mahogany doors were closed to keep out the draft.

"Is that you, Lexie?" her mother called out.

She slammed the outside door and locked it. She pulled off her mittens, took off her boots, and walked over to the hall mirror. Her face felt stiff. She touched it and then pulled off her toque as she stared into the mirror. *White as a sheet … I'm so white. I can't let them see me. They'll know something's wrong.* Her eyes looked enormous—brown and wild. She turned away, hung up her jacket, and threw her mittens and toque by the hot air register.

"Yeah, Mom." She cleared her throat and swallowed. "Good night."

"You're the last one in. Peggy and Giselle are sleeping, so don't wake them." As Lexie started up the stairs, her mother added, "Go right to bed now—and no reading."

"Okay."

"Have a good sleep," her father called.

If I tell them, they'll never let me go out alone at night again.

She tiptoed past Jeannie and Maureen's bedroom to the room she shared with Giselle and Peggy, who was fifteen now but seemed much younger. In bed she fell asleep almost immediately, face down with her arms around her head. In her dreams she was coming home, again and again; the man came from behind and bent over her. He smelled of wine and cigars now, like her father. *No. That's not right.* His bulk against her back was solid and heavy. She could see his arms. He wore her father's plaid jacket. He let her go, and she watched him stumble down the side street, a stranger again. He lifted one hand in a brown leather mitten and waved her away in dismissal, as if to say, "Get away! Scat ... you're not worth the trouble ... too stupid to run ... too stupid to answer me." All that night, her dreams continued. The blurred images of the stranger and her father bewildered her even as she slept.

Lexie was the last one downstairs for breakfast the next morning, tired and preoccupied with pushing away the dreams of the night. *Why is Dad in my dreams?* She looked past her sisters to him. He was eating porridge, carefully lifting each spoonful of hot cereal to his mouth. *He's not like that man at all.... He just pats us on the head, or sometimes a hug or a little kiss on the cheek. He'd never try to scare us.*

"Hurry up, Lexie, or you'll be late," her mother prodded automatically, not even glancing over to the table as she made sandwiches for school lunches. "Make sure Giselle keeps her toque and mittens on this morning. It's twenty below outside, and you know how she hates wearing that hat. And wrap her scarf around her neck and head before you walk home after school."

"I hate having to walk her to and from school. She never listens to me."

"She's just turned eight, Lexie. It doesn't hurt you to keep an eye on her."

There were three more evening choir rehearsals, and Lexie attended them even though she was terrified. She sat on the bus with her jaw clenched and her hands in fists. At her stop, she looked around before leaping off the bus and racing home. She burst through the front door, panting as she locked it behind her.

She no longer dreamed about the man catching and holding her. But Lexie watched men, even the boys at school. Her father patted her mother's bottom, and she saw the secret smile between them. And she noticed how the school superintendent leaned over Miss Bennet's shoulder, intimate somehow, when he was looking at reports on her desk. She brooded over, examined and re-examined, the way a sort of electricity had touched her when Garth, a boy she thought she might be in love with, accidentally grazed her fingers as he handed out papers that the teacher had given him. Their eyes had met, and the fingers touching had created the dark secret of sex. It seemed to be all around her. Even the priests knew. They often knelt down and hugged the little girls, but they only smiled and patted the arms of the older ones. And although they laughed and teased the nuns, there was no electric finger touching, no glances that locked and gripped for long seconds.

Lexie had different dreams now. They were fuzzy and uncertain, in clouds, with no ending. People were naked. It was all warm and musty in the dreams, and when she awoke, she was sick at her dirty mind and pushed these dreams away, too.

Lying back in the bathtub one night after Christmas, she slowly dribbled the water from her washcloth onto her stomach and small breasts. It beaded and ran down her sides. Her stomach ached. It was a curious sensation, a drawing downward on both sides of her abdomen. When she dried herself down around the new dark hair, the towel came away stained with blood. It frightened her briefly, until she realized that this must be the beginning of menstruation.

Some of the girls at school were already menstruating, and Mother had told her to expect it sometime soon.

This was confirmation that she was no longer the little girl her parents and older sisters thought her. She fixed herself with the pad and special belt her mother had put in the dresser drawer several months ago, along with a booklet titled *On Becoming a Woman*. Lexie had not looked at the booklet since then. Now she read it carefully and peered closely at the illustrations of the male and female body. For the first time ever, she examined her own body.

She thought about the man near the bus stop, about the frightening dreams that sometimes, without reason, had shown her father's face, and of her cloudy dreams of nakedness. Somehow she had to make some sense of all this. *I'm menstruating now. All this is sex. I'm part of it now. The priests and nuns pretend it isn't around, but it's everywhere.... I can feel it.* She put on her pyjamas and climbed into bed, feeling suddenly afraid.

She went downstairs for breakfast early the next morning, before any of her sisters. Her father was in the bathroom off the kitchen. Her mother was making toast and frying eggs for the family. Lexie told her that her period had begun. Her mother glanced up at her, continuing to butter toast and slide more bread into the toaster.

"Do you have everything you need?"

Lexie nodded and waited.

Mother handed her some warm toast. "Is there anything you want to know?" She had already turned away to the stove.

"No.... I guess not."

Her father joined her at the kitchen table just as Jeannie and Maureen came downstairs. Lexie looked at them. She admired them tremendously—they were both so pretty, self-assured, and successful. The telephone rang constantly for them, and their week-ends were a whirl of dances and dates. They hardly seemed to notice Lexie and couldn't be aware of how much she observed them and listened to their conversations, desperately wishing for their poise and sophistication.

After school that day, Lexie took a glass of milk, a plate of cheese, and an apple upstairs. She glanced into Maureen and Jeannie's room as she went down the hall. Jeannie was there alone; Maureen was still at school. "Hi, Lexie," Jeannie called, looking up from her book. Lexie was inordinately pleased. Usually if Jeannie was reading, she wouldn't notice anyone.

Suddenly shy, Lexie leaned against the door frame, balancing her snack on her library books. "Hi."

"C'mon in…. Can I have a piece of cheese?"

"Oh, sure … here." Lexie put the books down and handed Jeannie a wedge. She fell silent, striving to find something to say that would be worldly enough. "How's Robbie?"

"We broke up last night."

"Oh…. Are you okay? I mean, is it what you wanted?" She sat down on the bed next to Jeannie, who was stretched out, her book lying beside her.

Jeannie looked across the room and out the windows, ice-rimmed and frosted at the edges so they resembled old-fashioned oval glass. It was already dark outside. "I'll live." She reached over and took a bite of Lexie's apple. "What about you? You're awfully quiet lately."

"I started menstruating."

"What a drag."

"Yeah, every month for the rest of my life … well, until I'm old, anyway."

"We all have to put up with it ... can't have babies without it."

Lexie angrily threw her apple core on the plate and looked at Jeannie "That's crazy. Who wants to have a baby at thirteen? I bet you and Maureen don't want babies yet, and you're older. It shouldn't start until we're married."

"Linda Waller's going to have a baby."

"You mean Annie's big sister? She's in the same grade as Maureen, isn't she?"

"She has to quit school."

"Is she getting married?"

"No."

"What will she do?"

"Her dad said she and the baby can live with them. She'll go back to school next year, if her mom can look after the baby. But her mom's been awfully sick."

"Gosh. That's awful." Lexie shook her head in wonder. "Annie never said anything to me about Linda. I know her mom's really sick—we say prayers every day at school."

"Don't tell anybody about Linda. They'll find out soon enough."

"Is that why you broke up with Robbie? Over sex, I mean?"

"Hey! Mind your own business, Lexie." Jeannie smiled slightly to take away the sting. "Yeah. I guess it's part of the reason."

"Something happened to me just before Christmas," Lexie said as she picked up Jeannie's book, carefully turning a few pages.

"You mean with a boy?" Jeannie was instantly attentive, almost angry.

"No! Nothing really happened.... But maybe it could have. I don't know." She told her about the night she was walking home from the bus stop.

"You never told Mom or Dad?" Jeannie was amazed.

"No. Then they wouldn't let me go out after dark until I'm sixteen or something."

"It wasn't your fault. They would have called the police." She pursed her lips. "Gosh. You could have been hurt. ANYTHING could have happened."

"I know. But what could I have done?"

"Talk to Maureen. A guy tried to grab her when she was coming home from a movie last fall. She screamed and swore at him. He got scared and ran away."

"I couldn't make a sound. I couldn't move." *What a failure I am.*

"It can happen that way, when you're really afraid. But you always have to be careful when you're a girl, especially after dark. You can't daydream or dawdle. You have to look around, walk fast, get home quick as you can."

"It's not fair. Boys can go anywhere, anytime."

"That's the way it is." Jeannie looked at her watch. "I better go help Mom peel potatoes. It's your turn to set the table."

Lexie gathered up her books.

"Besides," said Jeannie, picking up Lexie's plate and glass, "not all men are like that. Dad isn't. Uncle Frank isn't."

"What about Robbie, or Linda's boyfriend?"

"They're not bad guys…. They would never attack a girl. They're just *guys.*"

"You mean whether they're bad or good, we always have to be the ones to be careful. Right?"

"That's about it. C'mon, Mom's expecting us."

"Don't tell her, Jeannie, about what happened to me."

"All right, but no more daydreaming after dark. You can never take anything for granted."

"I liked being twelve better," Lexie called out to Jeannie, who was tripping down the stairs, well ahead of her. But she knew this wasn't true. She thought about Garth, who today had asked her if she was going to the hockey game Friday night. She understood that if she said yes, he would take her for a cherry coke at the Blue Bird Café after the game, where all the couples gathered on Friday nights. It also implied that he would see her to her bus stop and very likely kiss her. She wondered if she would like it. She hoped so. But that would be enough, just a kiss on the lips in the dark near the edge of the street lamp's safety, with her bus coming along to take her home.

AN EVENING AT NICKY'S

"Toronto? Wow!" Lexie didn't know what else to say to Josie. Part of her was dismayed, felt abandoned—this was something that her capricious friend Maude might do—yet at the same time, she wished *she* had been so daring. "Toronto?" she repeated. "Back east?"

"Yeah! Why not?" Josie was so excited she could hardly contain herself. "I've never been there. But wouldn't it be a great experience?" She babbled on as Lexie chewed her lip. "And then if I like social work, I can get my post-grad degree at the university there. They have a good reputation."

"But what about Social Services here?" They had already been hired to begin after convocation in mid-May. Lexie had expected that they would continue on as roommates. But Toronto!

Josie shrugged. "The job here will still be waiting for me if it doesn't pan out in T.O."

"That's true," acknowledged Lexie. "Hmmm ... I could always join you. After a year or so, if I like the work, too." She was rapidly becoming more enthusiastic. "Have you got your flight booked yet?"

"No, I'm doing it tomorrow." Josie stopped and, as if reading Lexie's mind, exclaimed, "Say, do you think you could come with me now? We'd have a great time. My interview's on Saturday morning—we'd have Friday night and most of Saturday, and then fly home on Sunday."

"Gosh, I'd have to phone my parents and beg a loan until I start working." Lexie paused and then threw up her hands. "Oh well, what's another five hundred bucks in debt—I already owe thousands. It sounds wonderful—and we'd only miss one day of classes."

"Heck, let's fly out Thursday. We can afford to miss two days." Josie tossed a cushion from their ratty, second-hand couch into the air, and Lexie laughed.

"No, I can't. I'm having dinner with Maude that night—let's stick to Friday."

• ◆ •

Lexie and Josie shared an apartment in Winnipeg. They had met in their first year of university and had been inseparable since. Josie had grown up in the city and was living on campus only because her parents had moved away. Josie's poise impressed Lexie from the beginning. She saw her as a sophisticate, while she herself was only a rather timid Catholic girl from the country.

It seemed to Lexie that her life was pretty much settled. She would soon have her degree, and she was already assured a job. Keith, whom she had been going out with for nearly a year, wanted to marry her eventually. She always paused at this thought because she was not sure how much she loved him. Did she love him? Her parents liked him. He planned to study medicine after he obtained his undergraduate degree, and Lexie knew that her mother and father saw this as lifelong security for Lexie. But Keith demanded nothing from her that she could not easily provide. It was as if, she realized, he liked her better than she liked herself. Would this do, she wondered?

She hardly saw her Grand Coulee friends any more. Only a few had moved to Winnipeg to attend university, and they were all in different colleges. Maude, her closest friend, had moved to the city right after she dropped out of school, midway through grade eleven. "It's too dull here. I can't sit around all day any more," she had explained dismissively to Lexie. She had obtained work almost immediately as a nurse's aide at Winnipeg General Hospital and continued to live in the residence attached to the hospital for the cheap board and room. It surprised Lexie that Maude didn't show any interest in having an apartment and decorating it to her taste. Even on her own exceptionally limited means, Lexie enjoyed picking up little inexpensive objects to brighten up the basement suite she and Josie had moved into.

But she rarely saw Maude any more. They had different sets of friends. Besides, Maude slept around, and this made Lexie nervous. Sometimes the word *slut* appeared in Lexie's mind, but each time she quickly erased it. Never mind what was happening among the flower children of San Francisco, pregnancy was still the worst possibility for an unmarried girl from Grand Coulee.

Lexie was relieved when Josie told her that a single woman could get a prescription for the pill—the new and wonderful 99 percent safe method of birth control. She immediately got a prescription for herself. Then in the arms of her boyfriend, Keith, she could relax and explore sex. *After all,* she told her Catholic conscience—which still troubled her from time to time—*why was I given hormones if not for this?* She also decided she must pass this information on to Maude.

"Just make an appointment with a doctor—here in Winnipeg—not your family doctor," she had told Maude over dinner one night. "He'll give you a prescription if you tell him you're having trouble with your periods. Tell him they're all haywire, happening too often, unpredictable."

Lexie was very earnest as she gave this unsolicited advice, and Maude began to laugh. It sounded like silver bells tinkling, and several people looked up to glance admiringly at the beautiful young woman. But she either didn't notice or was so used to it that she didn't react. This was one of the things Lexie liked about her. "I've been on the pill for months now, Lexie. Quit worrying."

But Lexie didn't think she'd ever quit worrying about Maude, a quicksilver, lost, abandoned child whose mother died when she and Lexie were in grade one together. She went to live with her religious Auntie Joan because the father she boasted about—who travelled to exotic places like Montreal and Toronto and New York, and sent her wonderful presents—did not exist. There was only six-year-old Maude Carney, becoming tiny and tinier, it seemed, as Auntie Joan took over the management of her life. Throughout their school years together, they had been best friends. Maude, dainty and fragile, stuttering slightly, wearing her sweaters tighter as her breasts developed, was looking for love. Lexie had tried to save her. "Do you *want* bad things to happen to you?" she asked one day in exasperation.

Maude had answered, laughing lightly, "I just want things to happen, period. I get so bored."

• ◆ •

After checking into their Toronto hotel room, they shopped all afternoon, returning only to change for dinner. "So, are we going to Nicky's after?" Josie asked.

"Why not?" Lexie dug in her purse. "It's supposed to be a really neat bar, full of university types. I've got the address somewhere." She pulled out a piece of paper. "Here it is. It's near the university, Maude said."

The yeasty smell of draft beer and cigarette smoke, and the sounds of laughter, music, and loud voices enveloped them that evening at Nicky's. They assured each other that they looked terrific. Josie was wearing the outfit she had bought earlier in a too-expensive boutique—a miniskirt and matching pop-top the same deep blue shade as her eyes. Her pale blonde, straight hair hung past her shoulders, except for a few strands that always fell invitingly over one eye. She constantly brushed at them. She and Lexie had privately giggled over the sexy quality of this gesture.

Lexie envied Josie's long, straight tresses. Her own hair was a rich red and wavy. She had let it grow long to be stylish, but it always irritated her, and she usually tied it out of her way with a ribbon. That night, the ribbon was turquoise. She had made it from the leftover fabric after she shortened an old dress to just a couple of inches below her bum. Because she was petite, there had also been enough material to make matching panties. Hot pants were extremely fashionable—she was glad she thought to do this the night before they left.

They were also both wearing stay-up stockings, newly purchased and also very trendy. By 1968, garter belts and girdles were no longer necessary, and the stay-ups didn't have those annoying back seams. They had laughingly declared that this lack of seams to keep straight was symbolic, part of the great sexual revolution. That night, they were both pleasantly aware that lots of fellows were looking them over. So far, they had ignored all the interested gazes and casual comments, though they enjoyed the free drinks sent their way.

After an hour or so, Lexie leaned across the small table. "Don't be obvious, Josie, but there are two guys at the table over to your left. They've been watching us for ages. Mmmm … nice, too. They're older than most of the guys here. They don't even look like students." She waited as Josie casually turned and looked. The men acknowledged her and lifted their glasses. "What do you think?" Lexie asked. Maude did this kind of thing all the time, and nothing terrible had happened to her.

Josie raised her glass slightly in a mock salute to the guys. "Let's see how it goes. So long as we stick together."

They smiled up at the men as they approached. The one with thick, dark hair leaned over toward Lexie. "Hi. I'm Ross. Colin and I were wondering if we could buy you girls a drink." She indicated the empty chair. Ross sat down next to her, while Colin reached over to the next table, hooked a chair with his foot, and pulled it beside Josie.

Lexie liked the way Ross straightened his tie and pushed back his floppy hair before he spoke. "Haven't seen you in here before. Are you students?"

"No … well, yes we are. We just flew in today because Josie has a job interview. We're students at the U of Manitoba." She felt a bit shy, and fumbled for something else to say. These two men were well into their twenties and dressed in sports jackets and cord pants. She was used to Keith in his worn desert boots, blue jeans, and sweatshirt, sitting across from her in the student bar in Winnipeg, his heavy duffel coat draped over the back of his chair, books piled haphazardly in front of them. "What about you?"

Colin glanced over. He was already deep in conversation with Josie, but he paused to answer Lexie. "We're grad students—teaching part time in economics and working on our theses."

Ross ordered a round, hardly glancing at the harried waiter. He asked Lexie what she planned to do with her degree. An hour later, after several more drinks, they were all relaxed and easy with one another. Colin surveyed the group, and during a pause in the conversation, he casually suggested, "Why don't we go over to our apartment? Ross just bought the new Dylan LP." As an afterthought, he added, "And we've got some great hooch."

Josie glanced at Lexie, who gave an uncertain shrug. "Sure, for a while," replied Josie. Ross touched Lexie's hand. His was wide with brown hairs on the back that curled slightly. She stared at it a trifle too long and realized she was drunk.

The girls went to the toilet and stood side by side at the bathroom vanity. Lexie leaned over the sink and rinsed her mouth. Straightening up, she applied fresh, pale pink lipstick and watched Josie's reflection in the mirror, combing her hair. Josie caught her eye, and they talked to each other's images.

"Want to go through with this?" Josie raised one eyebrow and added, "I'm okay either way."

"Sure, I guess. They seem okay to me. Grad students in economics. Wonder what that means, anyway?"

"It means one of them may end up prime minister—and the other will manage the Bank of Canada. Or else they're lying psychopaths."

"Come on! I really like Ross." Lexie tossed her lipstick in her bag, and recalled how Maude had laughed at her cautious take on life. "What the hell," she exclaimed, quoting her friend. Even though Lexie sometimes suspected that Maude counted on her circumspection, it would still be fun to relay her own adventure for a change.

The drive in Colin's car took nearly twenty minutes. He drove fast, and after several turns, the girls had no idea where they were. They were riding together in the back, sliding drunkenly from side to side. Lexie felt like she might be sick, but they pulled up to the curb and stopped just in time for her to get out and inhale some fresh air. She felt okay again. She could see that Josie was gulping the night air, too, and this made her giggle helplessly. Ross took her hand and grinned.

In the apartment, several floors up in an anonymous high-rise, he poured generous glasses of his illegally purchased homebrew and stretched out on the floor next to Lexie. She was curled up, examining record jackets.

Colin was sitting with Josie on the nearby sofa. They were kissing. Lexie looked away, and Ross encouraged her to taste her drink. He told her he had watered it down for her with ginger ale. She hadn't noticed him doing this and realized that he was lying. This made her tense, but she smiled and obediently sipped as he watched with approval. When he rose a little while later to change the record on the turntable, she was glad and thought it would be a good time to leave. But then she saw Josie and Colin walking hand in hand down the hallway, into a darkened room. *That's Colin's bedroom*, she realized.

Before she could decide what to do, Ross picked up his glass and walked back to her. He lightly placed his hand on her thigh. She shivered slightly, and he took her hands and pulled her to her feet. They didn't speak. Lexie moved along beside him, dreamlike. She knew now that she was very drunk. She would have liked to lie down and sleep, but was unable to form the words to tell him.

Ross led her into his bedroom, and she stood silently, waiting. "You're so sexy." The sound was gruff in his throat. He undressed her, while she stood unresisting. The bed was soft; Lexie felt like she was sinking. It was too late to object. He kissed her hard and rested his weight on her. His chest and back were lightly covered with dark, twisting hair. She put her arms around him, digging her nails in through the tiny curls to the skin below. The only safe protest, she realized.

After he had finished, Lexie lay in the bed and stared at the chair across the room, strewn with their clothes. Her head was throbbing, and her mouth was dry. "I have to go. Josie will be waiting."

"She won't be waiting." He sounded bored now, replete. Lexie could barely look at him. She hated him. He watched her through half-closed eyes as she dressed. Her fingers fumbled at the buttons. Her stockings stuck as she tried to pull them on. Stretching languidly and letting his breath out in a soft rush, he too slowly rose, moved to the closet, and pulled on a pair of jeans. He followed Lexie to the living room and sat, head back, in the only easy chair.

The turntable had stopped. Their drink glasses lay overturned on the carpet. Lexie stepped over them and picked up her purse. She tried to think what to do. She was just about to gather her courage and walk into the other bedroom to get Josie when Colin came out. Josie followed and immediately picked up her purse, as well. The girls looked at each another as if to check that they were unhurt, and Lexie spoke first. "We'll call a cab."

"We could give you a ride," Ross offered half-heartedly, flipping his hair back. The gesture disgusted her now.

"No need," she replied, and they didn't object.

Colin phoned for a taxi, and as they all waited for it to arrive, an uneasy silence settled in. Josie half smiled and said, "Good luck with your thesis, Colin."

He blinked, as if he didn't remember having revealed so much about himself, or as if he didn't remember this lie. "Thanks ... good luck tomorrow."

The lobby buzzer sounded. Ross stood, tried to hide a yawn, and scratched his belly. "Cab's here. We'll walk you to the elevator."

In the cab, the girls didn't speak, until Josie whispered, "I've got this terrible headache." Lexie nodded and closed her eyes. She thought about Maude again and the risks she took almost on a regular basis. It occurred to her that Maude could die in some graceless pickup. She could meet a man who rapes and kills her if she changes her mind. This made fears about pregnancy almost frivolous.

By the time they reached their hotel room, they were both wide awake and sober. By tacit consent, they took turns showering—long and hot—and climbed into their twin beds. They fell into heavy, deep sleeps.

The next morning, while Josie attended her interview, Lexie wandered through Eaton's, hardly noticing what she saw. She wondered if Josie's head hurt as much as hers did. At least she was able to buy some aspirin, and it was beginning to help. They met at noon as they had arranged, at a coffee shop in the huge store. Josie couldn't stop grinning. She was obviously feeling better.

"They offered me a job on the spot doing adoption home studies. I start July 4th, after the long weekend. I'm terrified!"

"Oh, you'll be great. I know it." Lexie gave her a quick hug. "Congratulations. It's wonderful!"

"It's a huge responsibility, but I'll be teamed with an experienced worker for at least two months before I go out on my own, and they muttered something about training workshops." She paused to catch her breath and tried to calm down. "I had this moment of sheer panic just before the interview when I thought, *What if someone on the interview panel was at Nicky's watching us last night?*" She took a long sip of ice water and vowed solemnly, "When I move here, I will never, ever, go into Nicky's again."

Lexie nodded and grimaced at the thought of the night before. "I'm thinking of entering a convent myself."

They laughed, and Josie said, "We'll get over this. It's the sixties—everybody's doing it."

"Oh, not me. I don't want to go there again, ever."

Lexie wasn't referring to Nicky's in particular. She meant that place in her head, that point of sheer, dark recklessness, where Maude would go.

DEEP WATER

LEXIE SHOOK GERALD CANNING'S HAND AND FOLLOWED HIM from the reception room, through an open area where four stenos typed away, to his small corner office. She took a seat across the desk from him, and he handed her three typewritten sheets. "This is your caseload list," the supervisor began. "I'll run through it with you."

Lexie shifted her purse over her shoulder so that it rested on her hip, leaving her hands free. She looked at the first page. It was a series of names, addresses, and phone numbers with varied acronyms next to each entry, all of which had mysterious dates attached at the end.

"It's a rather large caseload," Gerald continued, "but some don't require as much attention as others." He began with the first name on the list and read it aloud, "Art and Jessica Gustafson. The AA stands for adoption application, and the date indicates when Shelley began the home study. A few items are still outstanding. They'll need to be completed before it's ready to submit for approval—individual interviews, reference interviews…." He rattled on. "If the reference lives in the district, see them yourself. Otherwise, you'll have to contact the social worker for that area to do it for you."

"Can I make notes?" Lexie asked timidly. "I didn't bring a notepad with me."

"Oh, sure. Marlene? … Marlene?" he called out.

An older woman in the steno area rose from her desk and joined them. He introduced her, adding, "Lexie's going to need another copy of her caseload list, and a logbook."

"No problem. I'll put them on her desk." And she was gone.

Gerald looked at his watch before he continued. "Your area, by the way, begins at the far south corner of the city and runs about a hundred miles southeast." Without pausing for Lexie to absorb this, he hurried on, racing through the first page. Lexie wrote like fury on the margins of her caseload list. *Oh, God, I'll never remember all this. Eighty-seven cases here! I've never even heard of most of these towns.*

"Sorry," Gerald announced, checking his watch again. "I've got to get going." They had only covered the first page of names. "I'll show you your office."

He introduced her to the other stenos as they walked through the area. "Mary Jane, here, will be your typist … and this is the file room." They entered a crowded room off to one side of the steno pool. "Marlene will explain the procedure for getting your files. You can't just walk in and take a file. They have to be signed in and out—and you must never take a file out of the building."

Lexie nodded. *He must really think he's got a dummy on his hands. I've hardly said a word.*

"Just a minute," interrupted Marlene. She picked up an envelope and handed it to Lexie. "Here are your car keys—the license plate number is attached—and keep track of your mileage. The office keys are in there, too. Be sure and lock up both the file room and main door if you're the last to leave."

Lexie nodded and thanked her before she and Gerald moved on, walking in and out of small offices on either side of a long corridor. He introduced her to the social workers who were not away on home visits. Finally they entered the last room at the end of the hall. "You'll be sharing this office." He nodded toward the first desk. "This is Bob Manley."

Bob looked up, nearly buried behind several piles of files and notes. He nodded and smiled. "It's Lexie, isn't it? I've got the caseload next to your area," he said.

"Hi." She walked over to the other desk. It was also piled with files, and the phone was ringing. She looked at Gerald.

"It's okay. Marlene will take a message while you get sorted out." He nodded to the piles on her desk. "These are a few of your files. Mary Jane typed the case summaries that Shelley wrote before she left. I'm not sure how up-to-date the rest are." He picked up a black binder, about six by four inches with tabs for each letter of the alphabet. "This is Shelley's old logbook ... for your reference. And here's your new one. Just enter each case like Shelley did and make a note of every contact you have with the client or any collateral."

"Collateral?"

"Collateral contacts, I mean. Like doctors, teachers, neighbours. It's important because you can refer to these notes in court cases."

We only got through the first page of the caseload list.... Oh boy. Still standing, purse over her shoulder, she tentatively opened a file.

"Well, got to go. Just ask Bob here if you have any questions about case procedure. And the manuals are over there." He nodded toward a bookcase. Then he was gone.

"And that's all you'll see of him this week," Bob intoned, a grin on his face. He stood up. "Sorry to abandon you, but I've got to be in court in ten minutes. See you after lunch. Marv's in the next office—he'll help you out." He stuffed his logbook and papers into his briefcase. "Oh, and you'd better answer any other calls, or you'll have Marlene on your back—she doesn't like too many interruptions."

Lexie continued to stand, unconsciously rolling and unrolling her caseload list, and glancing nervously at the phone. She leaned across the desk and examined the labels on the files. She leafed through Shelley's old logbook, hardly able to read the scrawled notes. Pulling open the top drawer of her desk, she saw an appointment book. She paged through it until she came to the present day. Three appointments were booked for her that afternoon. Two of the names she vaguely remembered from the caseload list. Frantically Lexie found their names on her list and deciphered the acronyms by each name. She looked them up in Shelley's logbook and began reading, her heart pounding. *What's the third name about, though? Is it a new case or one of those collaterals? At least they're all office interviews....*

She let her breath out in a whoosh, flushed with anticipation and fear. *I know nothing,* she thought, *nothing.* She turned from the desk and gazed out the window on the parking lot, wondering which of the government cars was assigned to her, wondering at the enormous task ahead of her. When the phone began to ring, she clenched her purse strap tightly. Finally she turned, tugged her purse off her shoulder, grabbed up a pen, and opened her logbook. *First of all,* she thought, *I'm going to need a map.* Tentatively, she picked up the receiver and swallowed hard. "Hello, Miss Doucette speaking...."

NO EASY ANSWERS

LEXIE MET FOURTEEN-YEAR-OLD VICKY FOR THE FIRST TIME ON a hot day in early July. They were driving together across the prairie, waves of heat rising above the fields and roads. The windows were open for air, and their clothes and hair and skin gradually covered over with fine dust. Lexie could taste grit in her dry mouth.

This was one of her first cases, and her supervisor, Gerald, had told her that the file should be closed as soon as Vicky returned home. It was to be a simple task. Satisfied that appropriate changes had been effected in the home, the court had ordered the child's immediate return. Lexie picked up Vicky in the city, where her foster family hugged her repeatedly before she got into the government car. They stood in the street, waving until the car disappeared from view. Vicky seemed excited at first, showing Lexie some of her farewell presents and saying she had promised to write to her foster sister every week.

But as they moved along, out of the city and onto the straight, grey highway that shimmered in the bright sun, Vicky began to cry.

She didn't want to go home. She seemed to believe that if she made her case sufficiently clear, Lexie would—could—turn the car around and take her back to her foster home. Eventually Lexie pulled over to the side of the road and tried to reassure her that things would be better at home now. Moreover, this was the judge's decision, which could not be altered.

Vicky's pale, freckled face was streaked with tears and dust. Lexie wiped at it with a tissue, and the girl clutched at her with damp, sticky hands. Vicky wept, talked, and wept again. She begged Lexie over and over not to take her home. But whenever she said she had no choice, Vicky would subside for a while, sobbing quietly, and then renew her pleas in the childish lisp she still retained—that lisp, the freckles, and the thin, small body all making Lexie feel protective, but ultimately helpless. She was just eight years older than this girl and three weeks into her first position. Social work was to be her life career, but she could hardly bear this. How, she wondered, did anyone stand seeing this pain? Could she do it another thirty years, like her predecessor Shelley had?

Lexie's supervisor had sent her to Vicky's house once previously, alone, to make the arrangements for returning the child to her family. Now, on this drive with Vicky, she couldn't sufficiently hide her own misgivings about the home that awaited the girl. Maybe, Lexie later pondered, that was how she had failed her.

The family lived on a farm three or four miles out from the nearest village. The house was a small, wooden, two-storey building. Inside, it was neat and clean, really nothing wrong at all. There was sufficient furniture—a couch and two armchairs facing a television set in the living room, with some ceramic ornaments polished to a high gleam on the end tables. But, as is the custom in most farm homes, they had sat at the kitchen table on that first visit. Across the room, she could see a toaster and an electric mixer set on the long, spotless, and otherwise bare countertop. Yet an all-pervading dreariness and sense of desolation prevailed. Vicky's mother had little to say, and when she spoke, she offered only terse, flat sentences that discouraged discussion. Years later, Lexie came to understand that Vicky's mother had detached herself from her family, probably because she could no longer afford to care; it was all beyond her ability to control.

At Lexie's insistence, the mother had called Vicky's brother down from his bedroom. Kenny was sullen, and after a glance toward Lexie, he stared out the window, responding in reluctant monosyllables when she attempted to start a conversation. He left the house as soon as Lexie released him.

Vicky's father hadn't come into the house at all. He wouldn't even come into the shade of the porch. It was as if that would have been a concession, an admission that the social worker had a right to be there. But as Lexie opened her car door to leave, he had called her over to his vegetable garden. Hoeing steadily and, like his son, refusing to look directly at her, he said, "You got my lawyer's letter. I been to court. You bring her back here. She belongs here." Then without pausing or waiting for her response, he talked about his cabbages, his cauliflowers, his carrots, about the shortage of water, and about the grasshoppers that plagued his garden and fields. He droned on endlessly.

It was hot and still in the garden, except for Mr. Wallace's unbroken discourse and the clicking of his hoe against the stones. Sweat ran down Lexie's neck and back, and she began to feel disoriented and dizzy. The situation was bizarre. She hadn't known how to handle it.

And so on that afternoon drive, she tried to comfort Vicky with words and gestures, like bringing her a pop from a gas station and wiping gently at her tears. She reminded Vicky that Kenny would be going away to school; he wouldn't bother her any more. But the child wouldn't be comforted. As Vicky whispered and sobbed, Lexie began to understand that in some ways she would miss her brother. He at least had noticed her, had been aware of her in that indifferent, lifeless home.

The court had ordered Vicky to be returned before she was ready and without any preparation, a further victimization, it seemed. The girl had been courageous—and desperate—when she had written a note to her teacher asking for help. Her brother was having sex with her, and she didn't know what to do. Her parents hadn't believed her, had shut her down when she spoke about it. Then they angrily denied the possibility to authorities. They had lapsed into sullen silence when Social Services acted after Vicky slashed vertically and deeply into her wrists.

Vicky grieved most of the long drive on that scorching day. She fell asleep just as they were approaching the town. Her light brown hair, which had shone and fallen freely to her shoulders when they started out, was now wet with perspiration and clung to her head. Her small skull looked vulnerable.

Before they turned off the highway, they stopped at another gas station. When Vicky went to the washroom, Lexie phoned her supervisor. She told Gerald how desperate Vicky seemed, and about her own serious doubts and how she hated doing this. He was sympathetic but adamant, reminding her that there was no choice: the court order was final—unless or until another incident happened.

Lexie pleaded again on the girl's behalf, but even though she could hear the regret in her supervisor's voice, the court order prevailed.

They got back into the car, but before they turned down the gravel road, Vicky clutched Lexie's hand and made her promise to meet her at the town café from time to time. She promised.

They drove into the farmyard and up to the back door. No one came out to meet them. They got out of the car and walked up the steps. Vicky pushed the screen door open. The kitchen was dim, and it took a few seconds for their eyes to adjust.

Mr. Wallace stood at the stove, pouring himself a cup of coffee. He was dressed in his work pants and suspenders, but he had no shirt on. He glanced at Lexie, but did not acknowledge Vicky, who stood silently, though nearly panting in her anxiety. "About time," he grunted. He sat down at the table to drink his coffee.

Vicky walked into the living room and across to her parents' bedroom. She looked in. Then she returned to the kitchen and glanced up the stairs toward her bedroom and her brother's.

"Where's Mom?" she faced her father, hostile and accusing.

"Visiting your aunt."

"She's not here?" Her voice shook. "When's she coming back?"

Mr. Wallace took a long sip of coffee before replying. "Tonight. The six-thirty bus."

Vicky looked over at Lexie. She lifted her hand as if to protest and then dropped it, uttered a small, despairing cry, and turned away.

Lexie tried to comfort her. "That's in about an hour—it's not so long." She turned to Mr. Wallace. "Kenny's gone?"

"Moved up to Winnipeg. Gonna take a mechanic's course."

She sat down at the table and motioned for Vicky to sit as well. Vicky watched Lexie as she spoke about the family readjustment and about the terms of the judge's order. She said she could be contacted at any time, that she would be pleased to help if any problems arose. Mr. Wallace drank his coffee silently and stared out the window, his chair tilted back on two legs. *How do you deal with men who won't listen to any woman?* Lexie wondered.

Finally Mr. Wallace spoke. "Where's her suitcases? She had two when she left here." Vicky and Lexie went outside to get them from the car.

"Stay until she comes. Please?" Vicky whispered urgently to her. Sighing inwardly—how she suddenly wanted to leave this misery behind her—Lexie agreed. But Mr. Wallace had followed them out and stood, arms akimbo, in front of the door. It was clear that only Vicky would be allowed back in the house.

There was nothing more to be done. Lexie got into the car and inserted the key into the ignition. Vicky reached her hands through the window and clasped Lexie's tightly. Lexie told her she would be in town at the café the next Tuesday at about three-thirty in the afternoon. Vicky nodded, stepped back from the car, turned, and carried her suitcases into the house.

At home that night in her small basement apartment, Lexie lay on her bed, exhausted but unable to sleep. Vicky's sobs and imploring voice still rang in her ears. Clenching her own hands into fists, Lexie could feel the girl's hands clutching hers; she could see the long, thin red ridges on her wrists. For the rest of the week, she checked constantly for telephone messages. There were none from Vicky or the Wallaces.

At the café the following Tuesday, Lexie took a booth off to one side, for privacy. Vicky came in with another girl a few minutes later. As she walked by Lexie's table, she hesitated, looked over at her without expression, and walked on. She didn't let on that she knew her. Lexie had been anxiously waiting to see her for nearly a week and had spent much of that time trying to convince herself that the girl was probably fine and glad, now, to be back in her home community. So when Vicky stared so blankly, Lexie had to adjust her welcoming smile. She looked down at her coffee cup, feeling her face grow hot and flushed.

When she looked up again, Vicky was seated with her friend in another booth further down, with her back to Lexie. After watching them for a while, Lexie began to understand what Vicky had conveyed so clearly in that deliberately blank look. *You have abandoned me.* She knew it was true, yet she could do nothing about it. Lexie waited a few more minutes and then left.

Lexie thought about Vicky often in the following weeks. Her case, along with others she was taking on, kept her awake each night. She wondered what would become of the girl. Would she successfully transcend her early isolation and betrayals? Would she become a busy wife and mother with a comfortable place in her community? Or had Vicky been irrevocably damaged, unable to sustain love? A woman who relived her emotionally destitute childhood while drunk or doped? And, in her catalogue of faces that have hurt her, would she include Lexie Doucette's?

Twice Lexie had to stop in the village near Vicky's house while on other cases, and she watched for a glimpse of the girl. But she didn't see her or her parents on the streets or in the café. She was still troubled every night with worries about Vicky and berated herself for not doing more. Why hadn't she brought the girl back to her office and let her make her own case to the supervisor? And, underneath it all, Lexie worried about herself. Was she cut out to be a social worker?

Six weeks later, she couldn't stand it any longer. It was mid-August, and after visiting a foster home in the area, she turned off the municipal road and drove down the dirt lane to Vicky's parents' farm. In the distance, at least a mile away, she could see a truck parked to one side and a swather slowly working in the field. She drove into the Wallace farmyard, parked near the back door of the house, turned off the ignition, and got out of the car. The place was totally silent. *Odd, this is the first farm I've been to where they don't even have a dog. No animals at all. Mr. Wallace is probably too cheap to spare money on dog food.*

She walked up the back steps and knocked on the door. No response. She walked around the house to the front door and knocked. Again, no response. She returned to the back porch and had begun to write a note to the Wallaces when she heard the sound of an engine roaring toward the house. It was Mr. Wallace, and he was driving like a madman, his half-ton careening from left to right as he cut a furrow through his nearest field of ripe wheat.

She came down the stairs to meet him. His truck came to a screeching halt just a few inches from where she stood. He threw open the door and leapt out, pushed past her, and raced into his house. Lexie stood there, shocked.

Within seconds he returned, holding a large gun aimed directly at her. "What the hell are you doing on my property?" he shouted.

She stared at the gun, not quite believing her eyes. *Two barrels. It's a shotgun,* she told herself.

She stepped back, raising her briefcase in explanation and as a kind of defence. "I—I brought the papers you need to reapply for

Vicky's family allowance and to get her reinstated on your medical plan ... now that she's home again."

Mr. Wallace stared at her. Lexie felt numb. *No use running for my car, that won't stop a bullet.* The only thing she was certain of was that she mustn't antagonize the man.

"She isn't home." He continued to point his weapon steadily toward her. "This isn't her home any more."

Lexie nodded carefully. "Has something happened, Mr. Wallace?" *Now there's a stupid question, you idiot!* But it was innocuous or silly enough to surprise an answer from the man. "She and her mother moved. Away from here." He lowered his shotgun and leaned heavily against the back door frame. "Out of this hell hole. As far away as they could get."

His voice was devoid of emotion. He could only be aroused to anger and hate these days, Lexie guessed. She felt afraid. The man was volatile, yet she had to know more.

"Where did they move to, Mr. Wallace? Do you have an address?"

She waited. He stared at her.

"Flin Flon ... the wife's got a job teaching." He shook his head. "Hasn't taught since Kenny—since before Kenny was born."

Lexie let out her breath softly. He hadn't shot her yet. "Do you have a mailing address? So I can forward these documents to ... to Mrs. Wallace?"

The man shook his head and turned to re-enter the house. "General Delivery oughtta do it. How the hell should I know?" he muttered. Then he turned to face Lexie again and shouted, "You people have destroyed this family!" He raised his shotgun and aimed. "Now get the hell out of here!"

Lexie got in her car and, fumbling with the keys, managed to start the engine. She backed up carefully, terrified of hitting his truck, and turned around. He never moved, his weapon still aimed at her. Heart pounding loudly, hands damp with sweat, she grasped the steering wheel, and as soon as she was out of his yard, tore down the road toward the village. She did not feel safe until the cloud of dust trailing behind her obscured the sight of Mr. Wallace and his gun.

When she saw a police car coming toward her, she pulled over and rolled down the window. The officer, whom she'd met before, pulled up alongside her. "You okay?" he asked. "Saw you driving down toward Wallaces'. Got a little worried."

"I'm fine."

"You talk to the old man?"

Lexie nodded. "The others have gone … Flin Flon, apparently. He had a shotgun … or rifle. I'm not sure."

Sergeant McNally shook his head. "Look, better follow me. My wife will make us some coffee. You need to calm down before you drive all the way home." When they reached town, they walked through the RCMP office and entered a side door into McNally's living quarters. An enormous police dog lying between the living room and kitchen rose and growled. McNally growled back. "Sit down, Sir!" He explained, "His name's Sir. He was a tough dude in his day, but he's retired now."

Sergeant McNally's wife glanced through the kitchen door, and he nodded to her.

"Phyllis, this is the social worker. Can you make some coffee?"

"Have a seat," Phyllis called, "and don't worry about the dog." McNally followed his wife into the kitchen, and Lexie sat on the nearest chair. Sir continued to stare at her, growling quietly. She tried not to look at him.

In a few minutes, McNally returned carrying a tray with two coffee mugs, cream and sugar, and a plate of store-bought cookies. "Coffee 'social worker black,' I take it?"

Lexie laughed and nodded.

"So what happened?" he asked, once they were settled with their coffee and he had taken over the couch, his long legs stretched out.

Lexie explained. When she was finished, he nodded. "Yeah, heard Mary Wallace finally got up the gumption to leave the old bastard. Nobody ever thought she'd do it." The dog heaved himself up and moved next to McNally's feet.

"It was her sister up in Flin Flon who gave her the gumption," interrupted Phyllis. She carried in a mug of coffee for herself and sat next to her husband. "She told her about the school there needing a grade-three teacher and pushed her into applying—back at the beginning of July when Mary was visiting her." She took a sip of coffee.

"Mrs. Wallace seemed like she'd given up when I last saw her," Lexie offered.

"My friend Marie Oudette—she's lived here all her life," Phyllis continued. "She told me that Mary came here her first year out of teachers' college. Taught here for two years and then married Artie Wallace. He'd just returned from Korea and was a young hero." Phyllis paused for a minute, staring into space. "Marie said they seemed like any young couple—happy, in love. She moved onto the farm with Artie—his parents had died and he inherited it, of course."

"I wonder what happened," said Lexie, keeping an eye on Sir.

McNally stirred. "He had nightmares and headaches—from his time in Korea. Still does so far as I know. And hard times, I guess ... scrabbling on that little farm to make ends meet. He made her stop teaching as soon as she got pregnant, so that income was gone."

"Yes," agreed Phyllis. "He became a bit of a tyrant. Wouldn't let Mary go out on her own. Never let the kids take part in anything. They went to school and right back home every day—no baseball, no hockey, no choir, nothing. We hardly ever saw them in the village during the summer, except on Saturdays, when Mary and the kids sold vegetables from that huge garden of hers. That was her and the kids' only spending money, I guess.... The other children thought Kenny and Vicky were kind of weird."

"But Vicky seems to have friends—I saw her at the café with a girlfriend a week after she got back."

McNally snorted, and Phyllis frowned at him. "Not really a friend," she said, "just a curious teenager, I think. Vicky didn't have any friends." She paused. "I saw Vicky in town a few times, too, after she returned home. I got the impression her father didn't care any more—I mean, he would never have allowed that before all hell broke loose a year ago."

"How did Mary Wallace get away to go up to see her sister in the first place, if he was so controlling?" Lexie asked

"She just up and walked to town, carrying an overnight bag, and caught a bus. Left him a note that she'd be back on the same day as Vicky." Phyllis thought about it. "She must have been desperate to do that after all those years of doing whatever her husband told her."

When Lexie had finished her coffee, McNally walked her to her car. "I'll go talk to him about the shotgun. I think that should be enough. He's never been a violent man."

NO EASY ANSWERS   79

"No. Vicky only talked about how strict he was."

Lexie drove out of the town, glanced at her watch, and decided it was time to go home—it had been a long day. *So, the mother took matters into her own hands,* she said to herself. *Well, that's a good thing—too bad she didn't do it years earlier. What finally made her do something?* She steered the big government car around the wide curved correction in the road. *At least I'm learning enough not to get myself shot—that's something.* She was too embarrassed to say it aloud, but she realized she was becoming a social worker.

LISTENING TO THE SILENCES

"YOU'VE LOST WEIGHT!" GASPED HER MOTHER. LEXIE WAS visiting for the first time since beginning her new job. "Social work is too hard. I knew it would be."

Lexie flushed. "Really, it's okay. I love what I'm doing." *Do I? Then why is it making me sick?*

In the bathroom, she weighed herself and discovered that she'd lost sixteen pounds. *Wow, I burned that off in seven weeks—seven weeks of sheer terror. It's got to get easier once I know what I'm doing.* She stared at her reflection in the mirror. *Maybe I'll never be any good at it.*

"Come on," coaxed her mother at dinner that evening. "You've got to eat." She heaped mashed, creamed potatoes onto Lexie's plate, along with two more slices of roast beef. "Trying to save drunks and addicts, perverts and wife beaters." She shook her head. "The people I feel sorry for are their poor children. What hope do they have?" She poured gravy generously over Lexie's dinner. "You're going to find out there's no helping some people."

"But, Mom, that's what the job is—children. Keeping them safe."

"Well, I worry about you." Her mother sipped her tea delicately. "You could have been a teacher or a nurse."

"There are enough teachers in this family," Lexie stated firmly. She took a bite of her meat. "And I have absolutely no interest in nursing."

Her mother sighed deeply, an art she had been perfecting since her marriage, Lexie suspected. "I read in the paper," she responded, "that a social worker got shot in New York City last week."

"Winnipeg's a long way from New York. The most danger I've faced is from a big, mean dog." This wasn't strictly true, but no use telling her mother about Artie Wallace and his shotgun.

On Sunday evening after driving back to Winnipeg, Lexie took her datebook out of her briefcase to check on her appointments for Monday—although they were already burned in her brain. The increasingly familiar knot of anxiety flexed in her stomach at the thought of the home visits she must make—to unknown places investigating allegations of child abuse. Lexie could see it all. Driving up to the house. Checking for dogs before getting out of the car. Knocking on the door. Facing suspicion, anger, threats, tears, drunkenness. Or a small child whose mother is still sleeping it off, the father long since disappeared. Talking her way in. Insisting on seeing the children separately. Checking out their bedrooms. Taking an inventory of the food in the house. Whatever was necessary.

During the night, Lexie woke from time to time, rolled over, adjusted her pillow. *Remember, notice everything and ask the right questions—you don't have to know all the answers, but you have to ask the right questions—and listen to the silences. Don't show fear. Don't back down ... oh, God. Get some sleep.*

At the office on Monday morning, before heading out to do her investigations, Lexie's stomach twisted again. A wave of nausea made her sweat, and she hurried to the bathroom, where she threw up. She had become quite efficient at it—leaning over the toilet bowl, vomiting and flushing simultaneously, then moving to the sink to rinse her mouth and splash her face with cold water. She could complete the exercise so quickly that no one in the office suspected that she vomited at least four or five times a week.

Her first call that day took her to the third floor of a large home, once very grand but now dilapidated, its yard strewn with spilled garbage cans, broken toys, and several wrecked cars. The house had been divided into tiny apartments with shared bathrooms. She peered uncertainly at the row of buzzers beside the front door. The names of the tenants were smeared, one was torn, another missing altogether. She took a chance on the one that might have been marked J. Butler. She waited. Eventually a young woman appeared through the glass, peeking down from the top of the stairwell.

"Come in. It's not locked," she yelled.

Lexie opened the door. "Are you Janet?" she asked.

"Yeah." Janet stared at her. "You from the welfare?"

"I'm a social worker, yes. From Social Services."

"Oh, Jesus." Janet took a deep breath and pulled her cardigan tighter against her chest. "Well, you may as well come in. I figured somebody would come around." She shook her head. "I knew that bitch downstairs would report me." She pointed at the front door Lexie was trying to close. "You gotta slam it or it doesn't shut right."

Lexie followed Janet down the corridor of the second floor toward the apartment. "But there's no reason for you to come." Janet's hands fluttered helplessly, her chin trembled. "I got nothing to hide."

The apartment door was open, and a child of less than two, wearing only a diaper, stood in front of it. She was sucking on a bottle containing a pink fluid. *What is that? Pop? Lemonade?* A large grey cat had insinuated itself around the little girl's legs. It was sniffing at her diaper.

"You're not s'posed to open the door, Ash." Janet pushed her back inside. "How many times do I hafta say it?" She looked around. "Jamie, didn't I tell you to look after your sister?" She stalked across the living room, past her son, and switched off the blaring television. Jamie, who looked not much older than Ash, began crying.

"Siddown." Janet pointed to a worn armchair. Then she pushed aside a pile of clothes on the couch and sat down herself, reaching for a cigarette smouldering on a saucer balanced precariously atop several movie magazines. "What did you say your name was?"

Lexie lowered herself into the armchair gingerly. The seat was damp. *I bet it's pee again. Will I ever learn not to take the upholstered chairs?*

"I'm Lexie Doucette. Here's my card." Janet read it carefully. "I understand that you're having some problems managing," Lexie began.

"I got no problems. No money, either." She stood up and grabbed Jamie, who hadn't moved from his spot on the floor and was still crying. "Here, I got a cookie for you and Ash. Take her into the kitchen while this lady and I talk." She coaxed her children into the kitchen as if they were small animals. They came only when she thrust the cookies at them. "Play with your toys. Go on now."

Lexie began again, but Janet interrupted her.

"She said I left them alone for two hours! That's a damn lie." She shook her head indignantly, the injured party.

"I can't say who called us about your situation, Janet, but we do need to talk about it."

"Look, I know it was that bitch Cathy Thiessen. I don't hardly know anybody else." She lit a fresh cigarette from the stub of the old and angrily discarded the butt into the overflowing saucer. Tears spurted from her eyes, and she wiped at them impatiently. "And I thought she was my friend," she finished bitterly.

"Tell me what happened that day. Last Thursday, wasn't it?"

Janet waved her cigarette in an arc and sighed dramatically, like any teenager trying to explain herself to an obdurate adult. "I had to buy milk for them, didn't I? I told 'em, 'Don't move—stay right in front of that TV.'" She pushed back a strand of long, lank hair from her face. "But there was a line up at the cashier's, and then I ran into a friend from my hometown, and we talked for a few minutes. I was gone … twenty minutes, tops."

"But the kids didn't stay in front of the TV. They were found wandering outside by the caller, no jackets and barefoot. It was only three degrees above zero."

Lexie watched Janet lower her head and stare at her hands. A silence fell. *Give her time.* She looked around the apartment. It was small and cluttered. Clothes were strewn everywhere, some stained, some possibly clean from the laundromat. Soiled diapers lay on the floor next to dishes with food dried on them. A few toys, dirty ashtrays. No sign of booze or drugs, at least. But that litter box!

"It must be hard keeping your place clean with two little ones." Lexie brushed the cat away, and it moved to the kitchen, lightly jumping on the table and eating out of one of the dishes, oblivious of the two children. "How many cats do you have?"

"Just Mattie, and the kids love her. They're real gentle with her." Janet glanced at the litter box, where feces were spilling over onto the floor. "I'll get new kitty litter when I get my welfare, but it's expensive, you know." She glared at Lexie. "Everything's expensive. How am I s'posed to live on what I get?"

"*Do* you have enough food for the kids?"

Janet dug a roll of toilet paper from the pile of clothes next to her and pulled a piece to dry her eyes. "I got some Kraft Dinner, but I'm outta milk, and I don't get my cheque for another week."

Macaroni. Is that it? "I need to check your fridge and cupboards, Janet." She moved to the kitchen.

Janet sighed deeply and followed her. "Maybe I can get something to tide us over at the food bank." Then she shook her head, frustrated. "But how am I s'posed to take the kids there on foot and drag them home again, plus a couple bags of groceries?"

Ashley and Jamie were at the table, sitting on torn chrome chairs sticky to the touch and greedily stuffing themselves with cookies. Ashley was sharing her cookie with the cat. Janet picked up the package and shook it.

"Jesus! You ate 'em all." She burst into fresh tears. "Now we have nothing."

The fridge contained some dried-up soup in a pot, a few crackers, and half a bottle of ketchup. The cupboards produced some flour and sugar, coffee, three potatoes, and a small bottle of pink medicine. Lexie picked it up and examined the label. "Is this what's in Ashley's bottle?"

"It's the only way I can get her to take it." She snatched the medicine from Lexie's hand. "Mixed with her milk. She's got a bad cough." As if on queue, Ashley produced a thick, heavy cough from deep in her chest.

Lexie picked up Ashley's bottle from the floor. "But look, Janet, the milk's curdled. It's sour." She placed her hand on the baby's forehead. "I think she's still got a temperature. What about the doctor?"

Janet gathered both her children into her arms and carried them back to the couch in the living room. "Look, how many times do I hafta tell you? I'm broke. I got no money!" She began to cry. "That means nothin' for bus fare. I can't get her to the clinic."

Lexie followed and sat next to them. "Do you have anybody who can help you?"

Janet hugged her squirming children harder. "No. I just moved down here from Dauphin two months ago." The children saw their mother crying again and began to wail. Janet soothed them with kisses and hugs, and finally released them. They ran off, back to the kitchen. *They're living on cookies and sour milk. God. But at least they aren't showing any signs of being afraid of their mother.*

"Don't take them away. Please. Sometimes Jamie's dad sends some money. Maybe today in the mail … I'll buy some groceries … take Ash to the doctor." She clutched Lexie's hands. "I love them. They got nobody else."

"Your family? Ashley's father?"

"Humph!" Janet lit another cigarette. "Ash's father. That's a laugh. Don't even know his last name. Worked for the carnival. Gone the next day." She flicked the ashes onto the floor, her hands shaking in distress. "Mom and Dad helped me out when Jamie was born, but when I got pregnant with Ash, they threw me out."

Eighteen years old. On her own with two kids. Where do I start?

"Let's take this one step at a time, Janet. Your baby's sick. She needs to go to the doctor. I can take you this afternoon, if you can get an appointment." She lifted a hand before Janet could protest. "That's number one. And I'll speak to your financial worker about getting you an emergency grant—enough to buy some groceries."

Lexie walked across the room and peered into the bedroom. A double bed and a cot. Blankets lay in untidy piles on top. No sheets or pillowcases. They obviously slept on the bare mattresses. Clothes and toys were strewn about the room, but it appeared basically clean. She returned to the living room.

"You're not going to take them away?" Tears ran down Janet's flushed cheeks.

Maybe I should.

"No, I don't want to do that. But you need some help. You know things aren't going very well, don't you?"

Janet nodded helplessly. "I just need some money."

Okay, do this right or you'll lose her.

"I think you're very lonely, Janet. You love your kids, but sometimes it's all too much for you. It's not just the money."

Janet broke into tears again.

"There are ways I can help you. I know you want to be a good mother."

Janet nodded, making eye contact, engaged.

"Will you work with me, accept some help?"

Janet nodded again, sniffling, almost laughing in her relief.

"There's a group of young women in the same situation as you are. They meet at each other's homes once a week, just to talk, share their experiences. Sometimes they help each other out with baby-sitting."

"It sounds good."

"You know you can never leave your children alone? Not ever?"

"Yes."

"And you have to clean this apartment up. Especially that litter box. You can always use some shredded newspaper temporarily." *She already knows she has to do it to keep her kids.*

Janet nodded, ashamed. "I get so depressed. Sometimes it's all I can do just to feed the kids and change Ash's diapers."

Well, she's talking to me. It's a start.... I'd like to put my arms around her. She needs her mother.

"We'll work on all that. Why don't you give your doctor a call now?"

Lexie left a few minutes later, promising to be back at two to get them to the clinic. *I think that went all right. But she needs so much. Did I do the right thing?... I'll give her until Thursday to clean up the place. Then if I keep checking on her every week ... maybe I can get some daycare for the kids, get her back in school. Yes, this could end well.*

She drove the car around the corner and parked it, leaving the motor running against the cold, raw morning as she made notes in her logbook. *Now, what's next?* She checked her datebook, relieved to see an address only a few blocks away. She glanced at her watch. *Jeez, it's eleven already!*

Bob and Kimberly Matchett lived in an aged four-storey apartment block made of red bricks. Long, narrow windows ran in symmetrical strips all across the building. Many of the windows had broken panes. More were covered in plywood or stuffed with blankets and newspapers. Very few had curtains or blinds of any kind. Lexie knew its reputation; it was referred to as "Fort Apache" by some of the ethnically insensitive locals. But she had never been inside the building before. She had been warned never to enter it alone at night—and to be on the alert in the daytime.

As she left the security of the government car and walked the pathway to the front door, she felt herself tensing. Two boys, about ten and eight, were riding their bikes aimlessly, without mittens despite the weather. One boy drove his front wheel into the other's bike. "Fuck off, cocksucker," the smaller boy complained. But when they spotted Lexie, they broke off their quarrel and began riding back and forth in front of her. She was forced to stop and wait for them several times.

"Who'd you come to see?" asked the younger boy.

"Some friends of mine," Lexie replied.

"Oh, yeah? Well what's their name?"

Lexie didn't answer.

"My mom's not home anyway, and neither is Sonny's."

The older boy, who apparently was Sonny, snickered, "Yeah. Mine's in jail, so she ain't no friend of yours."

What, is he living here all alone? She stopped. "So who's looking after you while your mom's away?"

"Fuckin' Petey's gramma, that's who." He pointed disdainfully toward the other boy. "I have to sleep with the damn little pisser. Eight years old and he still pees the bed."

"Do not!"

"No school today?" she inquired.

"No school today?" Sonny mimicked. "It's teacher meetings. Somebody has to tell them how to do their fuckin' jobs, don't they?"

Lexie laughed ruefully and shook her head. "You're a tough one, aren't you?" He smiled to himself at this and called to Petey, "C'mon kid, let's get those groceries before your gramma has a bitchin' fit."

By this time, Lexie had reached the front door. The security lock was broken, and the buzzers to the units were not functioning either. All that was left on the wall outside was a series of wires that had been pulled out, the dingy white of the actual buzzers still attached to some of them.

Lexie entered the front hall and looked up the first flight of stairs. The carpeting had been pulled off in patches, leaving bare, unfinished wood. Rancid smells of food fried in lard assailed her, along with an all-pervading odour of wine, cigarette smoke, urine, and years of grime. Several women were standing around. They looked at her suspiciously.

Lexie nodded as she passed them, and headed up the stairs purposefully. Number 206. She knocked on the door once, twice. She waited a few minutes and knocked again. Just as she was digging out her card to slide under it, the door opened a crack.

"Are you Lexie Doucette?"

Lexie nodded. "Kimberly? Kimberly Matchett?"

Kimberly slid the chain lock off and opened the door just wide enough for Lexie to enter.

"Did you bring the papers?"

"Yes, I've got them." Lexie followed Kimberly through the living room to the kitchen alcove, and they sat down facing each other across the kitchen table. "Here they are." Lexie pulled out the voluntary care agreements from her briefcase. "I think John got your kids' names and birth dates right—he's the intake social worker you spoke to yesterday. But check everything to make sure it's all correct." She handed the papers across to Kimberly, who began to read them carefully.

Lexie looked around. The living room and kitchen were as clean and tidy as she supposed they could be in this terrible old building. There was very little furniture, only an old couch, a television with rabbit ears, and the table they were sitting at with three mismatched chairs. She watched Kimberly. *She's beautiful. Absolutely beautiful. She could be a model or a movie star. Instead, she sits here signing away her kids for two months because she has cancer and she can't look after them.*

"John said you have no one to take the kids while you're in treatment?"

Kimberly shook her head. "Nobody. My mother died last summer, and she's the only one I'd trust with them."

"What about your husband, Bob?"

"I told John about him already."

"He just told me that your husband couldn't do it."

"I don't even know where he is. He took off a week ago. The police were after him." She looked up finally from the papers. "Anyway, I would never leave my kids with him."

"Where are the kids? Billy's three, isn't he? And Bobby Junior's four months old?"

"They're napping. Do you want to see them?"

Lexie nodded and followed Kimberly down the hall to the only bedroom in the apartment. Billy lay stretched out on his back, sound asleep on the double bed he apparently shared with his mother. Bobby Junior was curled up, fetal, in a crib so old that the bars were made of metal. The children looked healthy and clean.

"What beautiful babies—both of them," whispered Lexie.

Kimberly smiled for the first time. "I'm trying to prepare Billy for the move. Not much I can do for Bobby Junior, though. He's too young."

They walked back to the kitchen. "You go in the hospital next Wednesday, don't you? Why don't I set up something with the foster parents for Monday or Tuesday? I'll pick you and the boys up so you can all meet them. You'll feel better once you see where they'll be and who's looking after them."

"Thanks. I'd like that."

Suddenly Kimberly froze to the sound of a key turning in the door. A deep voice shouted, "Hey, Kimberly. Open the fuckin' door."

"It's Bob." Kimberly stood up. "Don't tell him what's going on. He'll be furious."

"I gotta get the rest of my stuff. Hurry up, bitch." Bob pounded on the door.

"I'm coming, I'm coming." She leaned over and whispered, "He won't stay long. I've got a restraining order against him, and he doesn't want more trouble with the cops." Kimberly hurried to the door, unlatched the chain again, and stood back. Bobby came in, followed by four or five other men. When they saw Lexie seated at the table, they stopped.

"What's going on?" Bobby's hostility was immediate. The other men slowly walked over and surrounded the table, staring down at Lexie.

The apartment was suddenly silent with menace. Lexie's hands clenched into fists in her lap. She concentrated on looking unconcerned, unafraid. She glanced at Kimberly, who hadn't moved from the door. No help there.

Still no one spoke, and the tension did not ease. *Get out of here. Just get out of here,* she told herself, sweeping all the papers together and stuffing them into her briefcase. "I'll come back later, Kimberly." She stood up and waited for the men to let her pass. It was several immeasurably long seconds before Bobby gave a silent signal, a slight tilting of his head, and the men moved just enough for Lexie to get past them. At the front door, she whispered to Kimberly, "Will you be okay?"

"Yeah, everything's cool," Kimberly answered loudly, looking back at Bobby and his friends. She opened the door, and as Lexie walked out, Kimberly whispered, "He won't hurt us. He's scared to."

"I'll phone you in half an hour?"

Kimberly nodded and shut the door. Lexie hurried along the hall, down the stairs, and out the front door. She hardly noticed the other tenants watching her leave. She was aware only of her breathing, taking the air in deeply and letting it out slowly as she unlocked her car and dived in. *Oh, Jeez. I'm such a coward. Should I call the cops? But nothing happened. She says she'll be okay.* Lexie started the car and drove off slowly. *If she doesn't answer or if she sounds different when I phone ... then I'll call the police.*

THE FEVER

ONE NIGHT IN BED WITH HER CLANDESTINE LOVER, BRUCE, Lexie casually mentioned that she was going to Harbour House the next afternoon. "Well then, you'll meet my ex-wife—the ice queen Cecilia. She's the matron there." Bruce paused. "Been there twenty years or nearly that." He rolled closer to Lexie, twined some of her long hair around his fingers, and pulled it to his lips to kiss it. "Just don't let on you know me, and you'll be okay."

Bruce was a professional painter who taught the night class Lexie had enrolled in as a way to meet friends in St. John's. Although Bruce was years older than she and had children nearly her age, he radiated vitality and enthusiasm. His voice was deep and rich, with an edge of laughter that seemed to suggest that the world—his world at least—was a wondrous place. His actions were full and sweeping, never hesitant or uncertain. Yet he was capable of gestures of intimacy as well, coming close and speaking softly, almost tenderly, to an uncertain student. Always a few fell hopefully in love with him.

After only a few weeks of classes, he began to show an interest in Lexie's painting. As he bent over her shoulder, she felt his sweater brush against her. She leaned against him, very briefly and very slightly. After class, he invited her out to coffee and the affair began. The class met on Thursday nights, when Keith, her fiancé, worked a late shift interning at the hospital. She was home, showered, and asleep before he returned. Sometimes at night she looked at him across the dinner table and wondered that he hadn't noticed any changes in her. She *was* changing, charged with a sort of simmering electricity from her encounters with Bruce. She told herself that this strange passion was a temporary aberration in her life that would surely pass, running its course like any fever.

She and Bruce progressed quickly into a liaison so passionate and sensually pervasive that she dropped out of the class to avoid embarrassment—otherwise the students would surely have noticed the sexual longing that passed between them.

They never contacted each other outside of their meetings, which continued every Thursday night, even after he had finished teaching the class. She met him at his apartment, where he was always working on a painting. He continued to dab carefully on the canvas while she sat waiting in silence, until he eventually sighed and dropped his brushes into the jar of turpentine, scraped his palette, slowly tightened the lids back onto the tubes of paint, and disappeared into the bathroom to wash his hands. Then he dimmed the lights and turned his attention to Lexie. She wondered at her own passivity during this ritual. She had felt unwelcome, an intrusion even, the first few times it had happened, until she realized that he was deliberately spinning out the thread of sexual tension that ran between them.

The relationship, if it could be called that, mused Lexie, was a secret that she held to herself, and if Keith sensed something, he was too absorbed in his work to explore it. But, as she drove out to Harbour House the next afternoon, she wondered if Cecilia had heard about it from some of Bruce's friends at the college.

Harbour House was located some twenty miles inland and south of St. John's. Set behind a thick, high hedge, the low grey cinder-block institution was gloomy, its deep-set, narrow windows spaced uniformly every four feet. In earlier years, it had housed up to forty-five patients, but now in 1970, the number was limited to a maximum of thirty, all of whom had been grossly brain damaged before or at birth. The residence had become not much more than an anteroom before death. The patients usually died—unmourned—before or in early adulthood.

Lexie had recently taken over a caseload of permanent wards, and most of her time was spent at foster homes working with emotion-ally damaged children. However, she was also responsible for more than half the patients at Harbour House, those who had been legally abandoned by their parents.

When Lexie buzzed the intercom and identified herself, an older woman unlocked and opened the door. She immediately knew the woman was Cecilia. The interior was silent and dim with the blinds half shut. Lexie was struck by an overwhelming smell of disinfectant, which only partially covered the sharp, acrid odour of urine and fecal matter, worsened by the overheated building.

Cecilia introduced herself, led Lexie into the sitting room, and pointed out a chair. Lexie sat. As Bruce had warned, she was scrupu-lously polite, but cold. "We'll have coffee before you see the patients." Then, in a tone that clearly implied that Lexie should have known, if only she'd applied some common sense, Cecilia remarked, "They sleep until two-thirty, you know, and can't be disturbed before then."

Lexie had promised herself she would not let Cecilia make her uncomfortable, but instead she found herself flushing and stammering, "I'm sorry. If I had realized that, I could have come later."

"No matter. I had presumed you would understand that they need afternoon rests. At any rate, this will give me time to familiarize you with our situation. As you know, you have sixteen of the twenty-two patients who are under eighteen years, and we also have eight older patients ranging in age from nineteen to twenty-three. We run three shifts of attendants." As Cecilia continued, Lexie watched her, listening on one level but thinking her own thoughts on another. *She's what they used to call a handsome woman. Big, but not fat. With a better haircut and some makeup ... but I can't see her with Bruce.... Look how affectionately she speaks of the patients—the first sign of a smile I've seen. And four kids to raise as well as this job.*

Lexie suddenly realized that Cecilia had stopped talking and was watching her with a slight, sardonic smile. *Oh, God. She knows. I'm going to be sick. I want to leave right now.* She managed a bland smile in return before glancing down at her watch.

"Yes. They'll be waking up now." Cecilia stood and brushed non-existent wrinkles from her uniform. Lexie followed her down a long corridor. She could hear the patients stirring. Some were crying. Others were moaning and making strange noises—guttural grunts and shouts that reminded her of schoolbook sketches of prehistoric men and of half-formed humanoids.

Cecilia opened the door to the hot, stuffy ward, trailed closely by Lexie, who shuddered as a new wave of stench—sweat, urine, and feces—hit her. Cecilia stepped aside to allow Lexie an overall view.

An attendant was opening the blinds. As the light grew stronger, she gazed up and down the long institutional room. Beds with railings were set at right angles from the two longest walls. As her eyes focussed on the inhabitants of the beds, she swallowed back the bile that rose to her throat.

Huge heads lolled on misshapen bodies that were naked except for diapers. Adult women whose breasts drooped to the edge of their diapers. Men with body hair, whiskered. Arms grasped and pulled uselessly at the metal rails of the oversized cribs. Faces gaped at her, drool running down their chins. They grunted and wailed and twisted their great moon faces into distorted grimaces. Some, who were blind and deaf, swayed and butted against the rails as they reacted to the light.

A second attendant, a wiry fellow in his twenties wearing hospital greens, brought in a trolley loaded with fresh diapers. Firmly, but not roughly, he held down a patient while the other attendant, a middle-aged woman, whipped off the soiled diaper and threw it into the garbage bag attached to the trolley. With practised hands, the woman, also dressed in green pants and a loose top, swabbed the patient's buttocks and genitals, wrapped a clean diaper around him, pinned it in place, and purposefully moved on to the next patient.

"Which are mine?" Lexie managed.

"I'll show you." As Cecilia led her from crib to crib, Lexie stepped back to avoid the hands that reached out to clutch her. But Cecilia bent over each crib and murmured softly to the patients, gently rubbing their backs. She briefly described each person's situation. Numbly Lexie took notes in her logbook in the hot, noxious room. Her fingers hardly worked. The cries, grunts, and occasional screams didn't stop until the attendants began passing out baby bottles filled with apple juice. The patients grabbed at them, sucking noisily and then breaking off to shout or bang the bottles against the wall and crib railings. They burped and coughed and snuffled as they tried to pull themselves up into sitting positions. But for most of them, the weight and size of their heads were too great.

"We'll put them, six at a time, in wheelchairs and take them for a walk a little later." Cecilia pointed to the chairs lined up along the far wall. "See. Special boards are attached, with straps to support their heads. Otherwise their necks might break."

This is the third circle of hell. How do any of them stand working here day after day?

"You get used to it after a while," Cecilia remarked, as if she was reading Lexie's young mind. "It's shocking to see for the first time. But someone has to look after these unfortunates. I suppose you wonder that we have them all together, age-wise and gender-wise, but we have limited staff, and the patients aren't bothered by it." They moved out of the ward through another door. "I'll show you the rest of the facility."

There was little else to see: a small bedroom next to the ward for the night attendant, two bathrooms lacking any accessories for the disabled ("We sponge bathe them in their cribs. It's too risky to get them into a tub"), a locked meds room, a laundry room, and a large, spotless kitchen. Soon Lexie found herself at the front door again.

"Thank you, Mrs. Fields, for your help. And thanks for the coffee." Lexie smiled tentatively at Cecilia, daring to make eye contact. "I'll arrange to come later in the day next time."

As she walked to her car and fumbled putting the key in the door lock, she could sense Cecilia watching her. She started the car and drove slowly around the semicircle out into the street. *Thank God I don't have to come back for six months—unless one of them dies, of course, and I have to make funeral arrangements.*

Before returning to her office, she pulled over to a coffee shop by a gas station. She sat staring into space, drinking her coffee and smoking as if to burn away the smell of Harbour House. She looked at her notes and was surprised to find that they were quite complete, with Cecilia's comments and even some of her own observations. *I can hardly remember writing them.*

Days went by. Thursday night came and went, and she didn't go to Bruce's apartment, though she was certain he was anxious to hear about her meeting at Harbour House. Images of the children and Cecilia hovered in her mind.

One evening while draining spaghetti, Keith turned to her. "How's the art class coming?"

Lexie swallowed. "It's okay." She drenched the salad with oil and vinegar, and tossed it busily.

"You haven't brought any paintings home for weeks."

"I'm working on a difficult one. I just leave it there to dry."

He shrugged and returned the conversation to his own passion—an endless discourse on his patients and his work.

The next Thursday night while Keith was at the hospital, Lexie telephoned Bruce. He answered on the first ring and chatted about his classes. He mentioned how busy he had been, as if he had been the one avoiding contact. A silence fell until he cleared his throat and asked her how the visit to Harbour House had gone.

"Fine … shocking. I hadn't expected them to be so … grotesque."

"Cecilia? Did she say anything about me?"

"No." She hesitated. "But I'm sure she knows about us, Bruce."

"It's possible. She's still in touch with a couple of the staff at the college." He added, without any inflection, "Some of them think I treated her badly."

"Did you?"

"It depends on your point of view." He paused, and she could hear him pouring something that was very likely the wine they always shared. "I got tired of it … the whole family scene in the suburbs … stifling … so I moved here a couple of years ago."

"I thought you'd been divorced for years."

"No, just two … but the marriage only half existed for years."

"Hmmm …" Lexie mused. "In your eyes, anyway."

"What do you mean?"

"Oh …" She thought for a moment. What did she mean? "I expect Cecilia worked full time, cooked, cleaned, looked after the kids, and entertained your friends. She *thought* she was married … and I imagine there were always pretty students in your life."

"It's true," he chuckled, pleased with this image of himself. "I'm better off without a family."

An image of Cecilia dominated Lexie's mind as Bruce talked. Tall and dark, with a sallow complexion and heavy circles under her eyes, and with the softening laugh creases around the corners of her mouth. She had been so gentle with the patients.

"Will I see you soon?" he asked.

Then she imagined Bruce in his living room, holding his glass of wine and sprawling languorously in the armchair near his easel as he waited—perhaps caring slightly—for her response. But he held no further attraction for her. With a start of surprise, she realized too that Cecilia's awareness of the affair had in it an element of pity for Lexie. When she thought of Bruce touching her now, it brought on the same shamed revulsion she had felt for the children at Harbour House.

She was astonished to discover that she wanted to gain Cecilia's respect far more than to keep Bruce's admiration. In a moment of clarity, she realized, too, that she must leave Keith, whom she had betrayed. She had to let him move on, as she set herself on a journey to honesty. She could only do her job honourably, like Cecilia, if *she* was honourable. She needed to go back to Harbour House soon—not in six months—and learn to accept the children's touch upon her skin. She must look into their opaque, dull eyes for a glimpse of sentience. And if that was not to be found, she must at least replace her abhorrence with compassion.

"Are you still there, Lexie?"

"Sorry, I was just thinking…. No, I won't be coming over any more. It's finished."

THE BALANCE SHEET

ONE MID-MORNING, WITHOUT WARNING, ONE OF LEXIE'S fellow social workers picked up her purse, walked out the front door, got into her car, and drove away. She never returned.

Lexie was on the telephone, just across the hall, and she saw her leave. Later she remembered feeling slightly puzzled; something had seemed not right. It was then that she realized Helen had not been carrying either her case logbook or her briefcase. Social workers always carry one or the other when going out on home visits.

But Lexie was busy—they were all busy. In this, her second year in St. John's, Social Services had experienced severe cutbacks, and social work caseloads had doubled. Whenever they gathered together, they all worried aloud and complained about the overload. They were already two weeks behind following up on intakes, except for the most critical. New referrals of child neglect or abuse remained nothing more than hastily scrawled notes beside their telephones. At first, they all promised to investigate each new referral the next morning. But after dealing with crisis after crisis and the never-ending paperwork, these promises were put off again and again. They soon learned not to make such commitments.

Very occasionally, someone would acknowledge the fear that consumed them all—their greatest fear—that a new child referred would be further brutalized or killed. They all knew who would be held accountable, and the ensuing investigation, whatever the outcome, would not alter their sense of failure. That fear was one of the things that kept each of them awake at night.

Days were filled with telephone calls, home visits, and consultations with doctors, psychologists, school staff, and foster parents. They coped with angry, resentful, and despairing parents; soothed frightened, damaged children; and confronted community members demanding quicker and better follow-up. For the children taken into care, there were foster home placements to arrange and court appearances to make, along with all the paperwork accompanying that emotional and legalistic action.

Each social worker reacted differently to the nightmarish pressure. Some workers withdrew and moved through their days unfaltering but detached. Others ran faster, became careless of their personal appearance, and made grim jokes. They all worked hours of overtime. A few, increasingly bitter and exhausted, resigned. Inexperienced young graduates eventually took their place. Although initially scornful of the anger and increasing hopelessness of their colleagues, the new ones became disenchanted frighteningly quickly.

Through all this, before she simply disappeared, Helen had amazed everyone. She was always calm, careful, and never seemed rattled, even in the most disturbing situations. She appeared quite willing to work late and often came in early. Her co-workers marvelled—when they had time—at her serenity, her unhurried approach to chaos.

They knew her caseload was as overwhelming as theirs, yet she continued to carefully assess intake after intake, make decisions, set up case plans, and prepare for court without apparent stress. Unlike Lexie and the others, she rarely expressed frustration or fatigue and always spoke in slow and measured tones. She was in control, and they all admired her.

On the morning she disappeared—simply picked up her purse and walked—she had been going through her phone messages and mail. Lexie, Janey, and Allyson, Helen's closest friends in the child protection unit, gathered in her office afterward. Lexie picked up a letter that Helen had crumpled and dropped on the floor near the wastepaper basket. She smoothed it out. "This is from Marylee MacLeod. You remember her?"

"Of course."

Lexie nodded, glancing down at the letter. "Yes, Helen removed her from an awful situation. I guess Marylee must have been about eight back then. She'd been abused—beaten, molested—severe neglect. Her mother had died of an overdose a few years before." She looked up from the letter and stared, focussed but unseeing, at Helen's desk. "Helen was very attached to Marylee. She saw her through years of therapy. Had to move her to, I think, three different foster homes before they found a couple who could cope with her behaviours. The girl had a rough adolescence. Cut her wrists when she was about fourteen." Lexie sighed and looked once again at the letter. "Did a good job of it, too. Nearly died."

"Wow," Allyson said, "this letter should go in her file, not the garbage. Helen could lose her job over that." She shook her head in dismay. "How old is Marylee now? What does it say?"

Lexie peered at the letterhead. "It's on the Calgary Foothills Hospital stationery. *Dear Helen, I bet your surprized to hear from me. Thoght you were rid of me, I gess. But they won't let me out of hear and your the only one that I know who can help me. Tell them its okay to let me out.*

The letter, nearly five pages long, was written in cramped, childish handwriting. Marylee had used a ballpoint pen with bright blue ink, and she seemed to have gripped it so tightly that the words were stabbed onto the pages. At times the ink had smeared, and the lines of writing ran across the pages haphazardly so that the letter, already nearly incoherent, was even more difficult to read.

Lexie glanced up. "Marylee moved to Calgary with her boyfriend about a year ago. She sent Helen a postcard—I remember Helen showing it to me. The girl sounded happy, and mentioned that she and Billy had got jobs and their own apartment." Lexie shrugged. "But I don't think she ever heard from Marylee again until this." She began reading aloud again. The letter was rambling and disjointed, but full of detail. They surmised that it had been mailed to Helen from the psychiatric unit of the hospital. *"Well, Billy got laid of. Couldn't find no work. He started drinkin again—and you know I already got a problem with that. I tried not to … but. Anyhow, he started to get real ruff with me. And I may as well tell you—you probly gessed already. We were shooting up again by then. Then the head bartender at Jake's were I worked came onto me. I told him to fuck off and he fired me."*

"It's the same old story," muttered Allyson, shaking her head. Lexie and Janey nodded. Lexie handed the letter to Allyson.

"You read the rest." She sat down heavily in the chair facing Helen's desk, the chair she remembered Marylee sitting in so often in the past.

Allyson continued reading. "*Well we ran out of money. Couldn't get no welfare. The bastard landlord thru our stuff onto the street when we were out job hunting.*" The three social workers looked at one another, knowing without a word that the couple had probably been shooting up again in some back alley. "*Billy rented us a room in a crapy hotel—just like the ones Mom and I used to live in. Funny how their just the same no matter what fuckin city your in. Then Billy dissapeared on me. Two days after I told him I was pregnant. Asshole. Asshole. Asshole.*" Allyson stopped and rubbed her eyes. "God. Your turn now, Janey."

"*What could I do? I had to eat, eh? So for a few months I did what my mother did. Got arrested but I was only in overnite. But by then I was getting huge, so I moved into a shelter until my baby was born.*"

Janey scanned a few more uneven lines of writing. "She had a baby girl. Called her Helen." She found a more coherent passage and resumed reading. "*I didn't leave no adress when we got discharged. Didn't want any nosy social workers in my life. So I took baby Helen back to that shity hotel and looked after her best as I could. Went out at nite to make money when she was sleeping. I always made sure she's sleeping.*"

Janey handed the letter back to Lexie, who read the final page. "She says one of the neighbours complained to the hotel clerk about the baby crying all the time." Lexie looked up. "Nobody gave a damn about the baby, of course, just that the noise was annoying them. Anyhow, the clerk phoned Social Services, and baby Helen was taken into care."

"Thank God for that," commented Allyson.

Lexie cleared her throat and continued. "*I knew I'd never get my baby back. So I jus didn't care what happen to me. I lived on the street for weeks. I got drunk and stayed that way. Sleeped with anybody who wanted it—I'd do it for a pill or a drink or a needel. I woke up here two weeks ago. A psych ward! Me! I gave the cops a hard time, thow. They had to restle me in here. Wish I could remember it, but the crazies in here said they had to drag me in and I was kicking and sweering. Punched one of the cops out.*" Lexie paused, squinting to make out the last lines. "It just gets more and more incoherent. It's all everybody else's fault.... *You got to get me out this nuthouse. Its hell. I don't belong here. You always helped me before. Please. Please. Please.*"

Allyson took the letter and stared at a word scrawled across the bottom. "This is Helen's writing. *Cancer.*" She looked at Lexie and Janey. "What does she mean by that? Who's got cancer?"

"Oh, my God," said Lexie. "I remember—" She shook her head. "Nobody has cancer. But Helen and I were talking a few days ago. About intervention and how the damage done to one generation extends toward another. You know how Helen speaks, measuring each word, stopping to pick just the right one. She said it's like a cancer metastasizing from body to body." She added, pointing to Helen's desk, "With all the other mail and the forty or so telephone messages that were waiting for her this morning, this letter must have just tipped the balance." Lexie looked around and fingered through the pile of mail. "She must have taken the envelope with the return address, though. That's probably what I saw her stuffing in her purse when she hurried down the hall this morning."

At about noon, Ken, the supervisor, cautiously asked if anyone knew where Helen had gone. No one had any idea. Her appointment book was marked with office appointments only. Several of these clients were sitting in the waiting room, growing increasingly impatient.

Ken picked up Lexie's telephone and dialed Helen's home number. "It's Ken Jackson here, Helen's supervisor. She came into work this morning and then left in a hurry.... She's home, then? Can I speak with her? ... Oh, I see ... Well, ask her to call me ... Thanks." He hung up, looking bemused. Shrugging helplessly, Ken turned to the social workers, who had begun to gather around him. "That was her husband. She's at home, but she couldn't come to the telephone because she's making bread." He smiled tentatively, the way he always did when he had no answer. "She might call back tomorrow."

Lexie had thought Helen's walkout might be temporary—for an hour or so—but to be home kneading bread! This was one of those moments when a preposterous, outlandish behaviour like Helen's seemed to be the only logical response to an insane situation. Lexie looked around and sensed that they were all, for a moment, envious of Helen. Some giggled uneasily; some welled up with tears.

Slowly Lexie and the others wandered back to their offices. As if it had been preplanned, they all sat silently for a few moments. They seemed to be re-examining their own responses to extreme pressure. None of them, Lexie believed, felt immune from a breakdown like Helen's. She wasn't even sure if *breakdown* was the right term, but she could think of no other. They were all paying the price with strained personal lives and ragged tempers. They became dormant, sluggish companions or frenetic pleasure seekers, and they burdened their partners and children with their weariness and anger.

As though they had made a resolution in unison, after that day they all began to work less unpaid overtime and made space for occasional coffee breaks together again. The job got no easier, but they relearned to put their cases away in emotionally sealed boxes at the end of each day, including the frustration of work not completed, of cases neglected. They often took the long route home to extend the break between work and their private lives.

That day was the last time Ken ever mentioned Helen's situation. He divided up her cases among the remaining workers, and they carried on. In the weeks that followed, Lexie heard that Helen had been living on tranquilizers. This explained her unhurried, unthreatened composure in the midst of constant, often conflicting demands, and accounted for her at times vague manner, which they had all mistaken for distraction—too many things to remember and do each day.

Helen never returned to social work. In fact, she steadfastly refused to come into the office again. Lexie couldn't picture Helen even driving past the building and imagined that she made elaborate detours to avoid the place. But after four or five months, Helen called occasionally. From time to time, she time invited Lexie, Allyson, and Janey for lunch at her home. They were always served her homemade bread, cold meat, and fresh vegetables from the garden. Social work was never discussed.

COMING HOME

LEXIE RETURNED HOME TO MANITOBA. AFTER TWO TURBULENT
years away, she had planned to be offhand and non-committal about
her time spent in St. John's. She was relieved, but faintly chagrined,
when she succeeded so easily. Her friends and family accepted her
news of the engagement she had broken off and the promotion
declined with a minimum of questions.

Lexie settled in Winnipeg. Social Services almost immediately
rehired her to the child protection unit. Her sisters Jeannie and
Giselle now lived in the city, too, and it began to feel like home.
Although her father had died a year earlier, her mother and Peggy
remained in the old house in Grand Coulee.

While visiting them one weekend, Lexie ran into Robin, a girl-
hood crush. He was alone, walking on the pebbles of the river's edge,
just in front of her. She was sitting with Peggy on a park bench. *He
hasn't changed much*, she thought. He still had that dreamy expression in his eyes, as if he were far away. Although he had grown tall,
he remained thin, with the tawny skin and blond hair that had first

attracted her way back in grade two. As she watched Robin picking his way among the stones, she remembered clearly her only date with him.

* ◆ *

One day, Robin had invited her to come to his house after school. Her mother gave her permission, and though Lexie felt shy and embarrassed, hoping no one would see her walking with a boy, she wanted to go.

He lived in the opposite direction from school to Lexie, and they walked on a trail through a small, wooded area. It was as near a forest as she had ever seen on the prairie. Even now, she remembered the scent of the drying grasses, the slight haze of smoke drifting from the chimneys of the town, and the golden poplar leaves floating down through the blue sky and slanting sun as they wandered along. Birds sang, and the world was hushed except for their chirping and trilling. Robin had held her hand. His was warm and dry, slightly chapped. Eventually, they emerged at his house on the other side of the woods.

The yard was enclosed with a barbed wire fence, but more than half the posts had fallen down, and the wire twisted and rolled around them. Chickens clucked and scratched in the soft dirt among broken bicycles, headless dolls, and toy trucks that had long since lost their wheels. Several old cars, their hoods up and trunks ajar, were crammed in. Three small children with yellow, coarse hair like Robin's were climbing in and out of the dusty, torn interiors, pushing squawking chickens aside as they scrambled out to greet their brother. When Robin told Lexie that he had thirteen brothers and sisters, she looked at the house in amazement. It seemed no larger than her own. Where did they all sleep?

As they entered the kitchen, Robin's mother, baby clasped to one hip, turned from the stove where she was stirring an enormous pot and stared. "Who's this?" she asked Robin.

"Lexie," he answered without further explanation.

She seemed satisfied with this and turned back to the stove. Lexie sat quietly on one of the long benches at the kitchen table beside Robin. The three dirty, noisy children from the yard joined them, and Robin told them to hush up. He handed Lexie an apple from the large bowl on the table. Immediately the other children jostled for apples as well. "Mind, only one each," warned their mother without turning.

Just as Lexie finished eating, an old lady Robin identified as his grandmother shuffled into the kitchen. She was dressed in a long black skirt and several sweaters. Her dry, white hair was loose and floating about her head in uneven wisps. Her back was bent, but her head was perched up top like an old clucking hen as she peered frantically around the room. Finally, she settled on Lexie. "Did you take my teeth?" she demanded.

Lexie managed to shake her head.

Just as the grandmother tottered toward her, arms raised as if to swat, Robin's mother intervened. "You left them in the living room, Mother. Look in your cup by the radio." She plopped the baby into its carriage by the table and took the old woman's arm. "I wish you'd keep those darned old choppers in your mouth. Come on."

"How can I when *she* keeps taking them?" muttered Robin's grandmother, glaring back at Lexie.

Robin and the three smaller children giggled at this, as did Lexie. They followed the women into the living room. Five or six older boys and girls were sprawled on the couch and across the floor, reading, playing checkers, and wrestling. She tried to count them all in her head, but they were all in constant motion. The radio played loudly. Robin's mother turned it down as she picked up a cup, plucked out a stained set of dentures, and popped them in the old lady's mouth. She issued various orders to the children and, like the chickens out in the yard, they scattered in different directions.

Lexie walked outside with Robin, regretful that she hadn't seen where all the children slept, though she imagined a room with tiers of wooden ledges like those in chicken coops, but with thin mattresses rather than straw. Robin walked her to the edge of the woods and pointed out the path she should take home. He never asked her to his house again.

● ◆ ●

Now, years later, as she watched him picking his way among the stones and mud, she called out impulsively, "Hello, Robin."

He lifted his head and glanced over. He seemed to recognize her and climbed the low embankment, walking toward them. Peggy sat still and silent on the bench, painfully thin and bent, while Lexie stood and waved at him. She was suddenly conscious of her own beauty, the beauty of her healthy youth—her waves of long, shining auburn hair, her large brown eyes, her firm tanned legs barely covered by her skimpy miniskirt. As Robin stopped in front of them, the sun caught his face, and he lifted his hand to shade his eyes. "It's Alexis

Doucette, isn't it? And you're Peggy." He reached over and shook Peggy's hand, smiling warmly. "I remember you."

Peggy responded in the blunt fashion that had so often embarrassed Lexie and her sisters in their teen years. "Well." She paused dramatically. "I don't know you." She turned to Lexie. "Don't know him from a hole in the ground. Who is he?"

Lexie smiled up at him. "It's Robin Hannigan. Remember? He was in our grade two class."

Peggy squinted at him in an exaggerated fashion and sniffed grudgingly. "Maybe I remember him." She stared at him suspiciously for a few seconds. "Did you stick a crayon up your nose once?"

Robin laughed and nodded his head. "Yeah, that was me."

Peggy laughed, too, congratulating herself for her good memory.

Now Robin gazed at Lexie. She flushed and flustered, grasping for something to say. "I remember Sister Margaret trying to get that blue crayon out with a pair of tweezers. You were so patient while she dithered. You never moved."

Robin walked with them to the Blue Bird Café and bought them cokes. He was living in Winnipeg, he told them, and taught at the university there. When Lexie told him she was living there, too, he asked for her phone number. She explained that she was a social worker, and he raised an eyebrow slightly, remarking that he supposed it was difficult work. Lexie smiled knowingly at the condescension in his tone. She had heard it before. She was familiar with this intellectual shuddering over the gracelessness of her work; it was different from the genuine curiosity of others. But it never really bothered her. She was committed to her work—she believed in it most of the time.

Weeks later in her apartment, after they had made love for the first time, she said to him, "You with the blue crayon—the colour of your eyes—stuck in your nose…. It's absurd, but at seven, I thought the waxy sky blue looked wonderful against your honey-coloured skin and yellow hair." She paused then and gazed past his shoulder to the ceiling above. "Funny … I'd forgotten through all these years that I fell in love with you that day."

But Robin did not remember Lexie's visit to his house and never confessed to any early attraction to her. Lexie found that he didn't seem to have any strong memories of his childhood, at least none that he wished to share with her. He rarely returned to Grand Coulee. "We're not a close family. I guess there were just too many of us." But he did keep in touch with Valerie, the second oldest, who had more or less raised him. When Lexie and Peggy met him at the river that day, he had only come home because Valerie had insisted. It was their parents' fortieth wedding anniversary.

He called himself Brian now. "It's my middle name, anyway. Nobody ever shortened Robin to Rob, so I made the change when I started university. Didn't want to spend the rest of my life as Robin. Got teased enough."

⚬ ⬥ ⚬

Lexie's mother was troubled by this new relationship. "He comes from a different background than you do … that poor mother of his … what kinds of people have fourteen children when they can't support more than three or four? And the priests were always pointing them out as the ideal family. What nonsense!" She shook her head. "They aren't bad people, Lexie. Just ignorant. You come from better than that."

This snobbery drove Lexie crazy. She sighed in exasperation. "This is Canada, Mother. It's 1972. Brian has a master's degree in English, and he teaches at university. Gosh, he'll be a full professor when he finishes his thesis. He has nothing to be ashamed about."

"He's bright, I agree," her mother replied reluctantly, "but he didn't have a normal childhood. I know you think I'm a silly snob, Lexie, but that *does* make a difference."

"Well, Mom," she replied, "I'm marrying him." She couldn't believe what had come from her mouth. She and Brian had never discussed marriage. Yet obviously, she supposed, it was in the back of her mind. How else had it popped out, fully sprung like that? There seemed nothing more for Lexie and her mother to say, or if there was more, neither wished to continue the conversation.

Lexie knew that despite the discordance of her marital life, her mother was lonely without her husband. Since his death, the house Lexie had grown up in was irrevocably different. Empty spaces occupied the most unusual spots: her father's chair, still holding the creases where he had sat night after night reading the newspaper; the sagging double bed of her parents' marriage, which her mother had exchanged for a single cot, prim with a white eyelet coverlet; and her father's tool shed, with spider webs covering over his hammers and wrenches. It made Lexie's throat ache to see her mother and Peggy drifting alone through the house, the silence covered over with the cold electric voices of television. She returned guiltily to her apartment. With Brian over nearly every night, she began to turn it into a home.

One Saturday night, three of her sisters came to her apartment in Winnipeg. Jeannie, now head nurse in obstetrics at the university hospital, brought Peggy in from Grand Coulee for the weekend and picked up Giselle from the university dorms. They ate homemade chili washed down with red wine and got giggly. They reminisced about their childhood and talked about Maureen, who was living in England with her husband and two children.

Finally Giselle turned to Lexie. "So tell us about Brian. Mom's going crazy. Says he's one of the Hannigans—whoever they are."

"No kidding!" exclaimed Jeannie. "One of the Hannigans? Wow, Lexie. Not somebody in *that* family!" She shook her head. "They all ended up nuns or priests or criminals."

"Almost true." Lexie giggled. "But Brian's okay. That's his second name. He was always called Robin when we were growing up. You must have had one of them with you in school, Giselle. There was always a Hannigan in every grade."

"You brought Maryanne Hannigan home once, Giselle," Peggy declared suddenly.

"Did I? Did she have red hair?"

Peggy nodded. "Yeah, really red. I hated her—she stared at me. Acted like she'd never seen anybody with a leg brace before!" She glared at the memory.

"Now I remember." Giselle paused and then declared triumphantly, "And you're right, Jeannie. She's Sister Mary Desmond now. She's in an English class with me."

The sisters tested Lexie to see if she could name all of Brian's siblings. She could. She recited their names in descending order: Donald, Valerie, Shannon, Gordon, Kenneth, Sarah, Barbara, Roxanne, Michael, Maryanne, Ted, Elizabeth, and finally, Pauline. She was less certain about their whereabouts, so she told them she'd forgotten. Her sister Jeannie observed that Donald was spending his life in and out of jail, Valerie had become a teacher, and Kenneth was a priest. Ted had entered a seminary, too.

Brian had been reluctant, almost angry, when she had pressed him to tell her about his family. He had been clear. "My mother is worn out. She watches television all day and goes to Mass every Sunday. My father finally retired from the CNR. We only used to see him every ten days or so anyway. He could hardly keep our names straight. Now he spends his time fixing up the house and yard. If only he had done some of that when we were growing up." He had paused and looked off into space for a moment. "Don't romanticize my childhood, Lexie. Seeing them once a year is enough for me."

But Lexie could not tell her sisters about this. It would be somehow disloyal. They might profess to understand his feelings and show sympathy to him for his unsatisfactory childhood. He could not have abided that. He would have been angry with Lexie for telling—his privacy was paramount.

He had finally taken her to meet his parents one weekend because, she admitted to herself, she had pushed him. The visit had not gone well.

Brian was distant with his parents, drumming his fingers on his thighs as he sat stiffly in a hard-backed chair. Lexie was left to make conversation. His mother was dishevelled, her brown, ravelled cardigan none too clean. She wore her husband's discarded felt plaid slippers and seemed loath to rise from her position on the old couch to turn the television down. Shaking his head, Brian finally crossed the room and lowered the volume—down but not off, Lexie noticed. She wondered if it was ever actually turned off. Mrs. Hannigan gazed at them with her watery blue eyes, but showed no more than the odd flicker of interest in their lives or in the lives of her other children. She spoke in a low monotone as if inflection would be too exhausting. "Shannon phoned. She's living in Saskatoon now. Got a job as a nurse's aide at City Hospital over there. Living with some guy." A silence fell until she stirred again and remarked, "Heard from Mikey. Says he's in Kelowna driving a cab." Lexie asked if he was married. Mrs. Hannigan nodded, her eyes glued to the television. "Yup. She's expecting their third."

Mr. Hannigan, too, showed little interest in Brian and Lexie, or in any of his children. Despite the lifetime free rail pass he received upon his retirement, Lexie noticed no talk of visiting the children, who had spread out from Manitoba as far as Nova Scotia and British Columbia, north to Churchill, and south to Los Angeles. When she remarked that retirement would be a good time to travel around, the couple glanced warily at her and shrugged. In the silence that followed, Mr. Hannigan offered to take Lexie out to see the improvements he had made in the yard. Brian stayed in the living room with his mother for a few minutes. Then he came outside and collected Lexie.

"I told you it would be no good. There's no point," Brian explained on the way back to Winnipeg. "He kept her pregnant for years, and she used up all her strength to bring us up." He cleared his throat and shook his head. "Most other people had enough sense to be a little deaf during the sermons on birth control." This reminded Lexie of what her mother had said about the Hannigans' ignorance. It shocked her to learn that Brian felt the same way. She didn't know what to say, and after a few minutes of silence changed the subject.

◦ ◆ ◦

Having stated her feelings earlier, Lexie's mother said no more, except that she was looking forward to a family wedding in Grand Coulee, even though they would have to plan carefully, mindful of costs. "I only wish your father were here to give his little girl away." Lexie missed him, too. She missed his deep voice and his casual arm around her shoulders or waist when they were standing together. She missed his unqualified approval, his masculinity in a house of women, and the look of pride in his eyes when he looked at any one of his daughters.

Brian, though, had been horrified at the idea of a church wedding in Grand Coulee, and Lexie finally acquiesced, knowing that her mother would be hurt.

It was then she realized that no matter how much he loved her, her love for him would always be greater. She accepted that no relationship was ever evenly balanced, but this was the first time she had been more giver than taker. She came to understand that Brian loved her as much as it was possible for him to love; he loved her smile and the secret curves of her body. And he admired her ability to connect with people, something he wasn't very good at. For Lexie, his lack of empathy made him somehow vulnerable, incomplete. Although she knew that he did not love her unconditionally, she understood that he needed her—she was someone who knew about his family but was not one of them.

Lexie adored Brian—his physical beauty, his intelligence, his drive for perfection. She liked that he allowed her to mother him—to cater to him in small ways: ironing his favourite shirt, baking apple crisps until he was tired of them, bringing him aspirin when he had a headache, anticipating his needs. She reasoned that if he did not love her as much or in the same way, it did not matter in the end. What mattered was that she loved him entirely, would give herself to him in every way, leaving her family behind if he required it.

They were married the weekend after Christmas in a civil ceremony at the Winnipeg courthouse. Brian arranged it all. Maude, Lexie's old school friend, and Jack, Brian's office mate, acted as witnesses. It would be years before Lexie could admit, even to herself, how cheated she had felt by this wedding.

Brian had given up his apartment and moved in with her in November before the wedding. After they had been married a few months, they moved to a larger apartment closer to the university. It took up an entire floor of a big old house and had two bedrooms, one of which became Brian's study. Their living room had once been the master bedroom and still retained the mahogany wainscoting and old brick fireplace. Lexie and Brian painted the walls pale gold to lighten the room, and the landlord provided thick gold shag carpeting. Brian hung prints he had acquired from the art gallery, and Lexie stained an old bookcase she brought from home. She kept her photo albums in it. She knew without asking that Brian would hate to see her family photographs scattered throughout the living room, but she allowed herself one small framed snapshot of her parents and sisters atop her bedroom dresser.

Their lives soon fell into a pattern. She continued her regular workweek, although she often did not get home until after six, while Brian's hours, for classes and his thesis work, were irregular. He liked to cook, experimenting with gourmet recipes containing exotic ingredients, which he tested on Lexie before inviting anyone else over for a meal. His friends became Lexie's, and she stopped socializing with her colleagues outside of work, except for an occasional drink when she knew Brian would still be at the university. She saw less of her family and Maude. This seemed natural to her now that she was married, and she was grateful that her mother and her sisters had the good manners to phone ahead to see if it was convenient before coming over. She did miss them, though, and on evenings when Brian was teaching, she often found herself over at Jeannie's apartment.

One Thursday evening, shortly after she and Brian had celebrated their second anniversary, she buzzed Jeannie's apartment. "Come on up. I've got a surprise for you." Jeannie sounded excited, but Lexie recognized something else in her voice. Anxiety, she guessed, as she emerged from the elevator. Jeannie was waiting at the door for her.

"What's up?"

"You'll never guess. Maureen's here. She flew out from London last night and phoned me this morning from the airport. She's got Jordan and Willie with her."

"What about Bill?"

"She says she's left him."

"No!"

Jeannie shrugged and whispered, "She's thin as a rail and the kids are crazy with all this. Everybody's exhausted, including me."

Maureen came around the corner to the entry. Her two young sons, aged six and four, skidded to a halt behind her. She and Lexie hugged, their eyes wet with tears. The boys stared at Lexie suspiciously. Jordan remembered her, but Willie had been just two when she had visited them in England.

They moved into the living room. Jeannie said she'd run bath water for the boys and make up the bed in the spare room. "I'll sleep on the floor in there, too," Maureen offered. "They don't want me out of their sight right now. "

"I could have brought the rollaway cot if Jeannie had phoned me," Lexie said.

"Oh, I think she's in a state of shock. Poor thing. I didn't mean to do this to her. But better her than Mom. I'll have to work up to that." She gathered up Jordan and Willie. "Bath time, boys. And then maybe Auntie Lexie will read you a story. Would you like that?"

The boys appraised Lexie. "No," they declared in unison.

Lexie giggled. The utter honesty of young children always delighted her. "I think it's going to have to be all you for a while, Maureen."

Maureen nodded. "Don't go away. We'll talk as soon as I put these mutts to bed."

They were still talking at midnight, even though Maureen had been up for nearly thirty hours. She told them of her growing dissatisfaction with the life she and the boys had led in London. "I felt so isolated. We could never get babysitters—we never had enough money for anything. So I stayed home, and Bill attended all those staff social things by himself. It made sense for a while—after all, he was the one working there, not me."

But it had not got any better, and she and the boys spent more and more time on their own. "Try living without central heat or enough hot water in that miserable damp climate. Half the time I felt like a character out of Dickens—chilblains and all. Bill got really annoyed with me. He, of course, never washed a single dirty diaper, but he sure complained about the smell of them drying. I had to wash them all by hand and hang them anywhere I could, all over the damned flat. They took days to dry. Tiny, bloody hole of a flat."

Jeannie and Lexie looked at each another. "We thought it was kind of cute, cosy, when we visited," said Jeannie.

Maureen glared at her. "You didn't come in January or bloody February, did you? No. You came in June, when we could get out of the joint all day." She started to laugh. "Oh, it's wonderful to see you, to be here. I'm sorry I landed in on you like this, Jeannie. I'll phone Mother tomorrow. I know she'll be glad to have us for a while, once she gets over the shock."

"What are you going to do?" asked Lexie.

"Get a job. I haven't taught for a while, but my degree's still good and so are my references. Mom kept writing about job openings in Grand Coulee Secondary, as if Bill would ever have moved there. He loves London." She shrugged. "Maybe Mom knew more than she let on. She didn't seem so happy when she visited last summer."

"Yes. She told us she was worried, that you and Bill didn't seem to be getting on," said Lexie.

"You knew, too?"

Jeannie answered, "We kind of guessed. We hardly saw Bill when we visited. He always seemed to be rushing off to one late meeting or another. We had hoped it would pass, or that we were wrong."

"I wish you *had* been. I spent a lot of time pretending it wasn't happening. He has a girlfriend, I know. And then one morning, I was trying to cram my grocery shopping into the lousy little useless refrigerator, and nothing would fit. I broke three eggs, and I started to cry. The boys were watching. I realized this couldn't go on. That was four days ago, so we're still in a bit of a state. But we'll make out okay now that we're home."

At one o'clock, Lexie glanced at her watch and stood up to leave. Maureen rose, too, and hugged her. "I haven't even met Brian yet, although I remember his family. Gee, you've been married over two years now." She stepped back and looked at Lexie. "How come you never wrote to tell me you're pregnant? When are you due?"

"What?" exclaimed Jeannie. "Are you really pregnant, Lexie? You never said a word!" She turned to Maureen. "You're observant. She *has* got a little stomach and her face is rounder…. Hey, Lexie, don't go!"

Lexie had turned toward the door, suddenly anxious to leave. "Yes. I am. Pregnant I mean. But I have to get home. Don't say anything to Mom. Brian and I are still getting used to the idea."

"Used to the—? It's about time! You must be well into your fourth month," exclaimed Maureen.

Lexie inhaled deeply, her hand on the doorknob. "I'll come over on Sunday, when Giselle's here, too."

Maureen and Jeannie watched her carefully. Lexie continued. "It's really late. Brian will be wondering where I am."

Maureen finally asked softly, "You're happy about it, aren't you?"

Lexie blinked in astonishment. "Of course. I love this baby. I feel like a mother already." She paused and added carefully, "It's a little harder for Brian. He somehow thought we could be married and stay forever childless, but I won't have it." She smiled and reassured her sisters. "Don't worry. It will be fine. Once Brian gets used to the idea."

Driving home, Lexie thought about the gradual disintegration of Maureen's marriage. She found herself comparing what she knew of that marriage with her own. She absent-mindedly held the steering wheel with her left hand. With her right, she massaged her upper left arm, where Brian had grasped her in his fury. It still felt tender, even though the bruises had finally disappeared. She remembered his anger as he shouted, "I told you I didn't want children!" He'd shaken her and continued raging, "I can't believe you would let this happen." He'd released her when she cried out, but he hardly seemed to register that he had hurt her. "I've had a lifetime of babies." He'd stormed into the bedroom, and Lexie had moved over to the armchair and curled up like a fetus. He returned within a few minutes, carrying his briefcase and a small weekend bag. "I'm going away for a few days." He apologized for shaking her. "I've never done anything like that before and I won't ever again. I'm sorry."

He was gone three days, the longest days of Lexie's life. She'd known that he didn't want children, but it was a fact she had discovered only after they were married. Would she have married him if she had known beforehand? *Yes*, she mused, and she would have hoped time would change him. Was that why she had occasionally forgotten to take her pill? Did she regret it? *Never*, she realized as she hugged herself fiercely.

When Brian returned, they established a silent, careful truce. Neither referred to the pregnancy. She understood that they would discuss the baby when Brian was ready.

Now, as she parked the car, she glanced up at their apartment windows. All the lights were out except for in the entry. That meant Brian had retreated to bed and would pretend to be asleep when she came in. She wondered what she would tell her mother and her sisters if he decided to leave her. A headline flashed across the front of her mind, banner style, in stark black and white: *Lexie Doucette: Alone Again.* Well, it would serve her right, she thought. She had always known how Brian felt about children.

The next morning was Saturday, two weeks exactly since she had told Brian about her pregnancy. She had hoped that by then he would understand her need for a child. The love she felt for him would not be thinned to a watery soup as it stretched to meet a child's need. But she knew that it might not be possible for Brian to believe this. Except for his sister Valerie's occasional affection, he had experienced indifference for too long in his childhood. He could not trust love. His only salvation, she realized, might be in staying long enough to fall in love with his child.

As they sat across the table at lunch, politely passing slices of cheese and cornmeal muffins, Brian looked into her eyes for the first time since the incident. "This apartment will be too small once the baby is born."

Lexie could have wept. She looked down at her plate, weak with relief and gratitude. He would at least try to be a part of this new family. She was careful not to be too emotional, though. "Yes," she agreed, "but there's no rush about moving. Is there?" She watched him as he rose and walked over to his briefcase. He opened it and handed her several sheets of paper.

"Take a look. It's the real estate office's copy—tells you the square footage, etc., on our new house. There's a photo, too. Although it's pretty grainy and hard to make out."

Lexie moved her plate away and put the papers down. "Our new house?"

He sat down again. "I signed the papers last night."

"Last night? You bought us a house last night?" *Without consulting me?* It was beyond imagination. She stared at him.

"You'll like it." Brian shifted uneasily, before adding firmly, "The baby has to have its own room."

"Not right away, surely," Lexie argued weakly. "Maybe after a few months."

"A month, yes, but we'll need our sleep. And the only spare room here is my study. You know I can't manage without it. This house is the only way."

So was this her punishment for allowing herself to become pregnant? Was this Brian's way of taking control?

In a matter of moments, she had moved from a state of dull dread and half-sickness to elation, and now, finally, to cold dislike and rage. She studied Brian's face for a moment. She told herself that she must let this pass. Make the best of it. For the baby's sake.

Finally she nodded in affirmation.

IN THE NEWS

IT HAD BEEN A PERFECT WEEKEND, AND LEXIE HAD HARDLY
thought about her caseload. Work was something she never discussed
at the cottage. As soon as the telephone poles and power lines disappeared—at the turnoff from the highway onto the gravel road that
led to the lake—she relaxed, knowing she would soon be safe in a
cocoon of sunshine and sand with her family.

No telephone, no television, no computer. Only a small battery-
operated radio that was seldom switched on. Other social workers
would have to cover emergencies; she was not even available for
a consultation. It was never entirely safe to spend the weekend at
home in the city. All too often, the on-call worker would contact
her to discuss a crisis with one of her cases, disturbing the balance of
her weekend by reminding her of what she would face on Monday
morning.

Now, on this serene Sunday afternoon drive back to the city,
the radio program "Cross Country Checkup" was interrupted by
a news bulletin. The body of eight-year-old Sarah Jean Yewell had

been discovered in the basement of a long-abandoned co-op store in Plaxton, a village twenty miles northeast of Winnipeg. The little girl had been sexually assaulted, beaten, and had apparently bled to death. The RCMP had taken the murder suspect into custody—an eleven-year-old boy. He, the reporter continued, was a neighbour of the small victim. The two children had been seen at the local swimming pool Friday afternoon, although not together. But they had left the pool at the same time, and the boy allegedly lured Sarah into the basement of the old store. In a steady, distanced tone, the reporter stated that after he had sexually assaulted her, he had beaten her around the head and torso with a rusted metal rod. The boy then returned to his home. The rod, an old poker now corroded with blood, had been found near Sarah's body.

Her parents had reported her absence to the police within a few hours. Most of the community, including the boy, had searched for her, and it was the local John Deere dealer who had discovered her body.

It hadn't taken the police long to identify the boy. Several children, when questioned, remembered seeing him talking to Sarah. The boy's mother told the police that her son had come home from swimming as usual and hadn't seemed upset. Then he had joined her on the back porch to help shell peas for supper. But when the police officer presented the boy's own swimsuit and towel, which had been found lying at the bottom of the stairs near the small body, he confessed to the murder. The reporter briefly concluded the story by noting that the RCMP had turned the boy over to the custody of Social Services. He had been placed in the security lock-up area of the Youth Detention Centre in Winnipeg.

Lexie looked out the window. Brian shook his head in dismay and turned off the radio. "Plaxton, eh?" He lifted his hand briefly from the steering wheel and pointed. "That's it up ahead. It looks so quiet. Who would have guessed?" He slowed the car down as they drove past. "Isn't Plaxton in your caseload area? Will you have to deal with him?"

Lexie gazed at the towering orange grain elevators that stood near the railway tracks alongside the highway, and at the few streets that comprised the village beyond. She released her breath slowly, surprised to discover that she had been holding it. She nodded her assent, her mind flooded with the image of the two children walking down the dusty street hand in hand, carrying their swimsuits rolled into their towels. Tomorrow she would have to go to the detention cells to meet this eleven-year-old murderer. She would get to know him and his parents, obtain psychiatric assessments, and make recommendations to a judge about his future.

Then she turned to her small daughter, secure in the back seat, and stretched out her arm to touch her knee. "Let's sing. What song shall we sing, Megan?"

VISCERAL PAINS

BY THE TIME LEXIE AND THE NEW SOCIAL WORKER ARRIVED at two in the morning, the police had cleared all the drunken visitors from the house. Broken bottles lay everywhere, and the sagging couch and overturned chairs were soaked with beer. The living room reeked of marijuana. Underlying that, a miasma of unwashed bodies, sweat-stained clothing, soiled bedding, rotting garbage, and faulty plumbing pervaded the air. The kitchen smelled of rancid grease. A few sliced potatoes were welded into a bed of congealed lard in a cast iron frying pan on the stove. A couple of bent spoons rested on another cooking element. Lexie took it all in with a quick glance. Cocaine now, too. Who got them into that?

Seventeen-year-old Gabey Magneson was passed out in a corner of the living room, a beer bottle still clasped in one hand. His left cheek was swollen and bruised. His father, John, grey hair lying flat against his skull and falling in stiff, oily strands below his ears, was shouting at the police officers as he staggered around the room in his stained cowboy boots. A crust of blood had formed around his nostrils.

More blood had splashed down the front of his plaid shirt, which had been torn in the fight, exposing his protruding stomach.

"You got no right calling the welfare," he bellowed. "Kids are fine. See for yourselves.... No right at all—makin' trouble for us." He kicked at Gabey to waken him, but the boy only moaned and rolled into fetal position. One of the officers told John to leave his son alone.

"He's okay," the officer reassured Marilyn, the new social worker. He bent down casually to check Gabey. "He'll sleep it off."

Gabey's mother, Darlene, peered at Lexie. After a few seconds, she nodded, as if to confirm that she was a familiar face. She tried to reassure Lexie. "The kids are alright, quit worryin' all the time." Then she engaged Marilyn with an anxious glance. "People just come over, we didn't ask 'em. They brought beer...."

She drifted off, seeming to have lost the thread of her thought. Her eyes were glazed, and she was having trouble speaking clearly. She held her hand over her mouth in an unsuccessful attempt to hide her teeth—one more had been broken off in the fight. Darlene was a tall woman, taller than her husband, but gaunt with long, stringy arms and breasts that sagged, pancake fashion, toward her waist. She may have been a pretty girl once, but now she looked much older than her thirty-four years. Her blonde hair was faded and frizzled from drugstore dyes and cheap home permanents. It stood out in wild clumps around her head, except for a bald spot on one side that looked red and sore—a result of the recent melee.

Lexie shook her head and responded to Darlene with a firm voice. Years of experience had taught her not to enter into arguments with drunks. "We're going to apprehend the children tonight, Darlene." She met her eyes until Darlene looked away, down to her own hands.

"No ... no, don't do that."

"You and John have to sober up and clean the house. It's not safe here for the kids."

"I'm cleanin' it up right now. You don't hafta take 'em away." Darlene began to stagger around the kitchen and living room, swearing and crying. "Seems like I'm always cleanin' this damn house. Damn kids. Nobody else does nothin' round here." She tried to clear the clutter, ineffectually moving bottles from place to place and kicking some of the broken glass under the couch. "Damn fuckin' social workers comin' into my house. Bitches!"

"It's not just tonight that I'm worried about." Lexie followed behind her. "This is the third time the police have called us out.... The teachers are worried ... and we've had other complaints, too. I've gone over all this with you and John, but the situation isn't improving."

"Fuckin' teachers! They're all troublemakers," shouted John. He was sitting on the couch, bent forward with his head in his hands. But apparently he had grasped what was going on.

Lexie turned to Marilyn. "I'll go check on the children. You stay here." She then looked at Darlene and asked, "They're all here, aren't they?" Darlene gazed away.

As Lexie walked across the room, a jolt of pain shot through her stomach—empty now from all the retching—and it reminded her of her husband's words earlier that evening. "I'm sorry, but you must have known I haven't been happy. I haven't been for some time." She had been astounded. Hadn't they worked through their problems months earlier? Eventually she had retreated to the bathroom, where she vomited again and again. It was only when the police had telephoned that she pulled herself together.

Now Lexie knocked and tentatively opened the door to the boys' bedroom. Thirteen-year-old Dwight was lying on a stained mattress, fully dressed but pretending to sleep. A beer bottle sat on the floor beside him. Eight-year-old Darcy was on the mattress, too, but he sat up and blinked at her as soon as she switched on the overhead light. His rib cage heaved and jagged with the pain of barely contained emotion, and she noticed that scars from an old case of scabies were still evident on his narrow chest and stomach.

"Hi, Darcy. Remember me? My name is Lexie." She leaned against the filthy windowsill and faced him. "I was here a few days ago."

"Yeah."

"It must have been pretty scary, what happened tonight."

"A little bit."

"Where were you when the fighting happened?"

"I hid in here." He began to cry. "Those guys were trying to hurt Mom. She was screaming and trying to push them off. But Dad and Gabey hit them."

"Your mom's okay, Darcy. But she and your dad can't look after you right now, so I've arranged for you and Dwight to stay at the Haydons'."

"I don't want to go away again," he sobbed. "What about Gabey? What's going to happen to him and Mel and Carrie?"

"Gabey's too old to come with me. He can look after himself now." *No he can't. But he's too old to apprehend.* She sat down on the mattress next to Darcy and put her arm around his shoulders. *God, he's gotten so thin, and he's so dirty.* Dwight opened his eyes and sat up. Lexie nodded at him before she continued. "There's a foster home just a few blocks from the Haydons'. I'm taking Melody and Caroline there. You'll be able to see each other all the time."

Dwight lit a cigarette stub that had been lying next to his beer. "Good. I'll be glad to get out of this fuckin' place. There's never any food around … and the old man beat on me again tonight."

Darcy interrupted. "He only hit you 'cause you took a beer. He said you're too young." Then he tried to reassure Lexie. "He don't hit us except when he's drinking."

Dwight shook his head wearily, and stood up. "Let's get going if we're going."

"Mrs. Haydon said she'd have hot chocolate and sandwiches ready," Lexie offered. "Dwight, could you help Darcy gets dressed and gather up your clothes while I get Melody and Caroline?"

"Darcy don't need no help." He closed his eyes briefly and shook his head again. "Aw, quit crying, Darcy, you big baby." Looking around the room, he mumbled in embarrassment, "Hardly no clothes to get. Mom lost most of them at the laundromat—they got stolen, I guess." *Poor guy, all the family shortcomings exposed tonight. He's humiliated.*

Lexie moved on into the bedroom that Melody and Carrie shared with their parents. It was a shambles, with clothes, toys, dirty diapers, and cigarette butts strewn across the old linoleum floor. John and Darlene's double bed, an ancient model with an iron bedstead, was pushed against the far wall. Across the room, next to a broken crib, ten-year-old Melody was sitting up on her bare mattress. She wore panties and an undershirt that were torn and grey, and was groping under the edge of her bed for her socks. She had already piled her blue jeans and sneakers next to her, ready for anything. Her eyes were huge in her face, and Lexie understood her fear in a new way. *I'm afraid, too. Of the unknown.* She tasted these words and felt their newness as she gazed at Melody. But in her mind, she saw her four-year-old daughter, Megan, as she had been earlier that evening, perched on her cot, fresh from her bath and dressed in white cotton pyjamas, her hair neatly combed and still damp. She was carefully turning the pages of a Dr. Seuss book as she waited for Brian to come and read to her. It was their nightly ritual.

Lexie sighed slightly, and Melody spoke. "You're back…. Are you taking us away again?"

"Yes, Melody."

"Am I going to the Levallees'?"

"No, I'm sorry. They moved away, Melody. But there's another family near the foster home where the boys will be staying."

Melody nodded in resignation. "I'll get my things." She picked up her jacket from the floor. "Carrie's diapers and stuff are over there." She pointed to the end of the crib, where the baby's clothes, soiled and fresh, were overflowing from a small cardboard box.

Melody and Lexie gazed down at eleven-month-old Carrie, who was sleeping with one thumb in her mouth, her other hand grasping a bottle of sour-smelling milk. Her diaper was soiled. "I just changed her a little while ago," said Melody anxiously.

"It's okay. I'll change her quickly." Gingerly she began to remove the old diaper. "Can you hand me a clean one?" The baby's buttocks were blistered and cracked, oozing blood and puss. Lexie sucked in her breath. She put the clean diaper on Carrie gently and wrapped her in her urine-stained blanket. The baby hardly stirred as she was carried across the room.

Shivering suddenly, Melody stopped and whimpered, "I'm scared … I don't want to go." Lexie reached for her hand, squeezed it gently, and pushed open the door. Dwight and Darcy were coming out of their bedroom at the same time.

Just as Marilyn saw them and started across the room to help, Darlene darted in front of her. Screaming incoherently, she pushed Marilyn aside and pulled Carrie from Lexie. The baby, now fully awakened, began wailing in terror.

With Marilyn shepherding the other children toward the door and the police officers standing impassively in front of John, Lexie peeled the screaming, panic-stricken Carrie from her mother's arms. Darlene's t-shirt stretched out in small, damp peaks where the baby had been clinging ferociously. It was an image that would haunt Lexie for weeks. At the doorway, she turned to call back to Darlene and John, "Come into the office tomorrow at one. We'll talk about everything then."

• ◆ •

Lexie's husband left her the next morning. Packed a small suitcase and said he'd be in touch. At intervals throughout the day—in between talking to her supervisor, the Magnesons, and a divorce lawyer; checking on the Magneson children; and beginning the extensive documentation required to apprehend the four children—she hurried to the staff washroom. There, she vomited again and again, splashed cold water on her face, and carefully applied fresh makeup. Her hands shook and her stomach ached, but no one suspected she was anything more than tired after working so late the night before.

At five-thirty, she picked up Megan from the daycare centre, took her home, and began an explanation about separation that she knew she would repeat many times. As though she had rehearsed this scene before, she reassured Megan that Daddy still loved her and that the reasons for his leaving were unrelated to her. Clearly puzzled, Megan asked, "Well then, doesn't he love *you* any more?"

During the next weeks, as Lexie prepared for the Magneson court hearing, she tried hard to reassure Megan that her world was still a safe place. The weekends, with Megan at Brian's, were the worst times for Lexie. Not knowing what else to do, she threw herself into her work, often spending all day Saturday and part of Sunday at the office.

• ◈ •

On May 21, 1979, a hearing began at the family court before Judge Patricia L. Timmins. The courtroom was empty, except for the small gathering at the front just below the judge's dais. On one side sat John, Darlene, and Gabey Magneson behind their lawyer, Lynne Wright. Howard Kostas, lawyer for Social Services, sat on the other side, with Lexie next to him.

Lexie was called to the stand and sworn in.

H. KOSTAS: *Ms. Doucette, on the night of March 7, 1979, you apprehended the aforementioned children and placed them in foster homes.*

A. DOUCETTE: *Yes.*

H. KOSTAS: *Besides the circumstances of that night, already known to the court, do you have any other information that led you to apprehend these children?*

A. DOUCETTE: *In addition to the notes I took after each contact with the family and others who were involved with them, I have transcripts of child welfare hearings from the provinces of Ontario and British Columbia, where the children have been previously apprehended and taken into care. In both cases, the grounds for apprehension were physical neglect and physical abuse.*

H. KOSTAS: *Anything else?*

A. DOUCETTE: *I am submitting the transcript of an earlier hearing and subsequent temporary committal of these children that was held here six months ago. I also have copies of psychiatric and medical assessments that were completed on the children over the last six weeks. They indicate that the two older children, Dwight and Melody, have been diagnosed with developmental delays. The tests are inconclusive for the two younger children. The medical examinations also indicate that the children are below normal weight levels. All the children required treatment for impetigo and lice. They also need dental work. The youngest, Carrie, required antibiotics for a severe diaper rash, which, unattended, had become infected.*

After a brief cross-examination by Lynne Wright, the lawyer for Social Services wrapped up Lexie's case:

H. KOSTAS: *Ms. Doucette, can you tell the court why you are asking for permanent committal of the children at this time?*

A. DOUCETTE: *Your Honour, this has not been an easy decision. I believe that John and Darlene love their children. But, tragically, they have not been able to meet their basic needs. Not just in the present circumstances, but over a long period of time—years, in fact. Both parents have received counselling for alcohol and drug abuse, attended parenting courses, and been offered respite care and daycare services for the children. They have had the services of teaching homemakers. Public health nurses have repeatedly visited the home.*

When the children were in care here earlier this year, the parents stopped drinking and complied with all the requests we made of them. However, within two weeks of the children's return home, we received reports from the police, the landlord, and several neighbours regarding drinking parties. We also received reports from the children's teachers about absenteeism and concerns regarding their physical condition. The children were coming to school dirty, improperly clothed for the weather conditions, and hungry. They had not been provided with lunches on several occasions.

Lexie glanced over at John and Darlene. They looked numb, and she knew they still had no real understanding of why they were there. They did not believe they were bad parents. A knot of pity for them at their public unfrocking sat heavily in her stomach, but she continued on relentlessly:

Dwight has told me that his father has punched him with a closed fist to the side of the head, over his ear and on his cheekbones, three times in the last year. His teacher confirms seeing marks that would correspond to these injuries; however, this was not reported to me until after I had apprehended the children.

Both Darcy and Melody have told me that their father has kicked and slapped them on several occasions, but they are vague about the time. They did tell me they had bruises and swelling on their legs from being kicked and on their arms and faces from being slapped. I could not see any of these marks.

Also, both Darcy and Melody wanted me to know that these things only happen when their father is drunk. John denied to me that he had ever struck or kicked the children. Darlene, however, admitted that she has seen John kicking and hitting the children when he was drunk. She showed me her mouth, which is missing several front teeth, and indicated that John knocked two of them out when she got between him and Melody.

Lexie reviewed her notes, took a sip of water, and concluded:

We do not believe, based on past history, that the situation for the children will be improved if they are returned home. We are also greatly concerned that if the children are returned, the Magnesons will leave the province so that follow-up supervision and monitoring will not be possible. We believe it is in the children's best interests to be made permanent wards.

H. KOSTAS: *Thank you. Your witness, Miss Wright.*

Lynne Wright rose to request a three-week adjournment to give her time to review the evidence and to obtain rebuttal witnesses. She also pointed out passionately that her clients were making every effort to improve their situation and that they loved their children dearly.

DARLENE MAGNESON: *We can still visit the kids, eh? Lexie's been taking us over every week.*

JUDGE TIMMINS: *Anybody have any objections? Right. Parents to continue to have supervised access to the children at the discretion of Social Services.*

Over the next three weeks, as the resumption of the adjourned hearing loomed, Lexie juggled her time between continuing to comfort and reassure Megan and do her job. Pain and anxiety settled in her viscera, and she felt nauseous most of the time. Vomiting, which had always been her reaction to stress, became a daily, recurring part of her life. She spent many hours with John, Darlene, and Gabey, explaining again and yet again her reasons for seeking permanent guardianship. Initially, the Magnesons had been angry and abusive, but as the reality of court date grew closer, they became less combative. They collected months of accumulated beer bottles for refund and purchased a second-hand vacuum at a flea market with the cash. Darlene bought sheets and covered the filthy mattresses, and John repaired the broken railings of the crib. Proudly, they gave Lexie a tour and begged her to reconsider.

They enrolled in a substance abuse treatment program and, desperate to stay sober until court, obtained prescriptions for Antabuse. "But you know Antabuse only works when you take it all the time," Lexie pointed out. "Remember last time? As soon as you got the kids back, you stopped taking it and began drinking again."

"No, no. This time we'll keep on it. No more drinkin'. Not any more," Darlene assured her.

"It's important to keep your counselling appointments. Antabuse is only a temporary solution. Counselling and AA will have long-term results."

"Antabuse works good," John declared.

Lexie drove them to visit the children once a week. On one occasion, she brought the children to the office family room and left them to meet privately with Gabey and their parents. After an hour, she opened the door slightly and gazed at the family. John had the children sitting in a row on the couch. They had all removed their shoes. He had a handful of old shoelaces. He knelt in front of the children and carefully measured each child's foot with one of the laces, placing a knot at the tip of the toe and another knot where the lace touched the back of the heel.

He glanced up at Lexie and explained, "Gonna buy them new shoes for court. Never noticed how wore out their shoes was."

Lexie nodded. "That's a good idea."

The children looked up and gravely stared at her, and then turned back to their father. *A moment of love. But he'll disappoint them again.*

Soon after that, during meetings with Lexie, John and Darlene began to reveal their ambivalence about returning to court—and about the children themselves. "I don't think that judge will give 'em back to us. Too many things happened." After she said this, Darlene looked at John for his nod of affirmation before she continued. "I don't know. Maybe they're better off where they are." And they began to reminisce about the children as if they had already lost them.

"Remember when we took them to the midway? They sure loved the rides, eh?"

John nodded. "Yeah. Darcy got lost." He laughed and shook his head. "He was just a little bugger then."

This show of bravery as they confronted their failure and loss made Lexie's throat thicken and her stomach tighten with anxiety. She wondered briefly why she did this job. *It's for the children,* she reminded herself.

The Magnesons came back to Lexie's office on June 8, three days before the hearing was to resume. "We had a little party the other night," John began confidentially.

Darlene leaned forward and interrupted, "Yeah. See, we only invited Wes and Irene. We was already drinking with them. But then all these others showed up. Never even knocked. Well, some asshole started a fight and the neighbours must have called the cops."

"Three cop cars showed up. Sirens going an' all." John's voice rose in amazement. "Turned into a real brawl. Darlene there, she hit a cop." He looked over at her in admiration. "It was accidental, though, but we got arrested. Spent the night in jail, but they didn't lay no charges. Then when we got back home, the landlord was waiting for us. Gave us an eviction order." Darlene nodded in confirmation.

"We made a decision," John continued. "We sold all our stuff, except these things that belong to the kids." He handed Lexie two shopping bags containing a few clothes and broken toys. "No more court. We're not gonna to fight no more. It's no use. Kids are better off."

Darlene wiped her eyes with the tissues Lexie had handed her. "It's too late," she said, "John threw away the Antabuse and bought beer." She shrugged, gesturing helplessly with her hands. "It just happened."

Lexie took them out for coffee and they talked some more. Lexie urged them to stay for the court hearing, at least. But they followed her back to the office, determined to sign the necessary consent forms that day. "Gotta ride first thing tomorrow morning," John explained. "We're leaving for sure. Might get some work in the Okanagan pickin' fruit." They promised to write to the children, care of Social Services. At the last moment, just before Darlene hugged her, Lexie pulled a new package of twenty stamps from her purse and gave them to her.

The court hearing lasted less than fifteen minutes, and the four Magneson children were made permanent wards of the province of Manitoba.

A few days later, Lexie finally went to see her doctor about her constant nausea and vomiting. She reminded him that she had always had a delicate stomach and had thrown up before every exam at university. And during her ten years as a social worker, she had vomited two or three times a week, always before or after a tense situation. But now—and she began to cry—since Brian had left her, the pain was continuous and there was blood in her vomit. The doctor ordered some tests and prescribed medication for ulcers as well as a muscle relaxant. Reluctantly, she accepted a referral to a counsellor—one whom she did not know professionally—and took a two-month medical leave from work.

It was a year before Lexie saw the Magnesons again. She happened to be standing in the doorway to the reception area when they arrived at Social Services. She watched as they straggled in, one after the other, as though connected by a safety line.

John came first, his long hair greyer now and hanging to his shoulders. He walked as she so clearly remembered—shuffling, his head bent toward his feet as though marvelling that they still moved in their cracked old cowboy boots. He wore the same plaid lumber jacket, and his blue jeans, blackened and stiff with grime, still hung below his large stomach.

Darlene followed him—long, raw-boned, with washed-out dried yellow hair hanging in clumps around her face. She wore a torn pink t-shirt, and her sagging breasts appeared to be tucked into the waist of her long faded floral skirt. The hem drooped unevenly just above her dusty sneakers. She peered around and ahead with quick darts, ever anxious for what might befall.

Gabey came in last. He had grown since Lexie had last seen him. He was thin, and still moved awkwardly, as if unused to his long legs and big hands and feet. He seemed as good-natured as ever, looking curiously around him and shyly smiling at the others in the waiting room while John spoke to the receptionist.

Lexie moved away from the entry before they caught sight of her. She waited in her office for the call from the receptionist. It didn't take long. "The Magnesons have come in to apply for transient aid. There won't be a financial worker available for an hour, so they're wondering if you can see them while they're waiting."

They greeted Lexie like an old friend and followed her to her office. Soon it began to smell as it always did when they came in—the same as the pervasive odour in their house over a year ago: stale beer and unwashed clothes and bodies. "The kids liked getting your postcards," she told them. "They wanted to write back, but you didn't give return addresses." The messages had all been similar: *Dear kids, we are in Thunder Bay* (or Swift Current, or High River, or Surrey). *Might get work here. Hope you are being good. Love Mom and Dad and Gabey.* Lexie guessed that the work rarely materialized, or if it did, they quit after a few days, once they had accumulated enough money to party.

"Yeah, well, we was on the move all the time. You know, from job to job. Never knew where we'd be next," said John.

148   DEANNA LUEDER

"How are they? What's Carrie look like now? I bet she's running all over the place," interrupted Darlene, leaning forward eagerly.

Lexie told them about each child. "You know, if you're going to be in town for a couple of days, I could arrange a visit."

They glanced at one another tentatively before Darlene responded. "Yeah. But see, we got a ride west waitin' for us if we can get a little money for gas and food. We can maybe get work pickin' sugar beets in Alberta." She hesitated. "I'd like to see them, but …"

"You know, I'm looking for an adoption home for them."

"Yeah, we know. You said you would be …" Her voice trailed off, and the room was silent for a moment.

John stirred in his chair and nodded to Gabey to stand. "Well, guess we'd better get goin'. Maybe that other worker can see us now, get a little start-up money."

Darlene stood as well. "You tell them we was asking about them. Tell them I'll write again soon's we get to Alberta."

Lexie knew there would be no more letters.

She walked with them to the reception area. She remembered how they had parted last time. John and Darlene, weeping, had both clutched her hands before they left for the road. Her own eyes had filled with tears as they shared with her a few moments of their pain, of their grief, and the poignant acceptance of what had happened to them.

They had all made hard adjustments over the last year. She and Megan had accepted their own loss, and Megan was beginning to feel secure again. Lexie doubted that she herself would ever feel secure.

An hour later, she glanced up from the paperwork she was doing and looked out her window. The Magnesons were just leaving, walking toward a half-ton truck parked nearby, where a young man waited in the driver's seat, smoking a cigarette. They stopped beside the truck to examine the cheque they had been given.

For the first time that day, Lexie saw Darlene from behind. A large patch of menstrual blood had stained the back of her pale skirt. It must have been there for some time, because the skirt was stiff where the blood had dried. She watched them climb in the old truck and drive off down the road.

BLINK OF AN EYE

LEXIE AND HER SUPERVISOR, JOAN, WERE WALKING DOWN THE hallway outside the Social Services office, on their way back from the public washroom, when they noticed something on the door leading to the reception area.

"Look at that!" Joan exclaimed. They peered at the thick red letters smeared on the plate glass.

"It's lipstick," said Lexie. "What does it say?"

Joan examined it. "I can figure out *some* letters...."

Lexie peered closely at the scarlet print and began to decipher. "*I'll get you, Dom.* No, *Dor. I'll get you Dora Rob ... Dory Robertson.* It must say Dory Robertson."

When they entered the reception area, Dory, a senior social worker, was also surveying the scrawl. "That's Sally March's work."

"Yeah," interrupted Janelle, the young receptionist standing behind the counter. "I saw her sneaking out of here when I came back after lunch. I checked the datebook, but she doesn't have an appointment."

"This is the fourth or fifth time she's done this kind of thing since Monday," Dory added. "There's more on the back hallway wall, too." She shook her head. "I have to call Martina again—her mental health worker—but they're so short-staffed. I've left several messages."

Janelle shuddered. "It's kind of scary, isn't it?" But the three social workers just shrugged and walked down the hall to their offices.

"What's Sally got against you, Dory?" asked Lexie.

"I had to apprehend her daughter, Michelle, last weekend. Martina phoned Friday afternoon to say she was concerned because Sally seemed to be having a psychotic episode—talking to herself, withdrawing. They hospitalized her, but she must have been released almost immediately.

"How old is the child now?"

"She's six. A sweet little thing." Dory shrugged. "Usually I put her in the same foster home each time Sally has an episode, but it was full up, so everything is new to her.... She's not handling it very well—frightened by her mother's behaviour first and then turned over to complete strangers." Dory shook her head.

"You're seeing her today?" asked Joan.

"Yes, after school—I'll pick her up there."

"She'll adjust," comforted Joan. "But this cycle is becoming more like respite care. You'd better check that budget, Dory. I think it's running low."

"Budgets, budgets, always budgets." Dory paused and added thoughtfully, "Usually Sally calls me herself when she senses an episode coming on—she's very responsible that way—and it's a co-operative effort. This time was different. I took control of the situation by removing Michelle without Sally's consent. Just added to her sense of paranoia. I went to her house yesterday, but she wouldn't let me in."

• ➤ •

Later that day, Lexie picked up her daughter at her after-school program.

"We built a snow fort," Megan announced. "But we got cold, so we had hot chocolate instead."

Megan drew a picture of the fort after dinner, chattering on about how it had been built. "And then Jason, he threw a snowball and teacher told him, 'No snowballs, Mr. Epps.' Isn't that funny?" Megan giggled and explained, in case her mother didn't get the joke, "That's Jason's other name—Epps." Lexie smiled and laughed in all the right places, and even managed a question or two, but her mind was on Sally and Michelle March.

Why does this happen to Sally? She shifted, drawing her legs up onto the couch. Sally's voices must have told her to stop taking the drugs. Maybe they told her she didn't need them any more, so she stopped and her paranoia grew worse. Lexie pictured Sally in her tiny apartment with her daughter: pacing the floor, pulling the curtains tightly closed, shutting herself from public scrutiny to talk with her voices. Maybe Michelle grew afraid of her mother's ravings, of her face twitching, frowning, and grimacing unnaturally as she reacted to what she alone could hear. Maybe Michelle began to cry.

"Mom ... M-o-o-ommy! The phone's ringing."

Lexie started at the sound of Megan's voice. "I was daydreaming, I guess." Brian was calling to arrange a time to pick up Megan for his weekend with her. Then it was Megan's bath time, and Lexie gave her full attention to her daughter while she tucked her into bed, read her a story, shared kisses with her, and turned out her light. It was only when she returned to the kitchen to wash the dishes that she began reflecting on the past year and a half.

When Brian moved out, she and Megan had remained in the house. But Lexie soon found that she no longer felt safe there. She was fine in daylight or even when her daughter was up and running about. But at night in the darkness, when four-year-old Megan lay sleeping, Lexie imagined possibilities, wondered at every sound, hardly slept. She took to keeping a pair of scissors under her pillow. Finally she decided to sell their home.

She received enough from the sale to buy a bright, new condominium close to her office, and with a school nearby that offered after-school care for children of working parents. With its security system and neighbours close by, the condo felt safer to Lexie. She reasoned that it was more important that Megan have a mother who was not half mad for lack of sleep than to have a swing in her own backyard.

While Brian seemed to be enjoying his single life a great deal the second time around, Lexie's own life had become circumscribed—or more focussed, as she preferred to put it. There was work all week and Megan to be cared for. But Brian took their daughter every second weekend, and Lexie had slowly learned to fill the empty hours with grocery shopping, housework, reading, and visiting her sisters.

At first, it had taken her a long time to make small decisions—to plan a meal, to buy a sweater (*He liked me in blue, but what do* I *like me in?*), to choose a book (*I prefer fiction, damn it!*)—without automatically considering what Brian's reaction would have been. A sense of freedom and confidence came back to her with each decision made, each time she laughed and enjoyed the trivia of daily living without censure.

She weighed Megan's trauma against Michelle's, but there was no comparison. Megan, she told herself, has two sane parents who love her. Michelle has only her mother, her unpredictable, sometimes loving, sometimes alarming mother. Sally, pacing and muttering, frightened and angry. Did Sally feed her daughter regularly when she was like that? Did she bathe her once in a while? Dory said Sally had once set her own hair on fire because her voices told her to do it—*oh, God, if Michelle had watched that, how terrified she would have been.* What a confusing world the child must live in, never knowing what would happen next. Lexie shook her head.

Stop it! You can't dwell on the terror of every child's misfortune. She put the last dish away and wiped the kitchen counter. She tried to comfort herself with the knowledge that she and her colleagues tried to do something for them, at least. *Still, Sally's lost her daughter again, and we social workers are the enemies who take her away. Maybe we should call the police, too.*

At noon the next day, as she passed through the reception area, she called to Janelle, "I'm going home for lunch. See you at one." On her way out, she noticed a fresh lipstick message written in the hallway that led to the elevator. She didn't stop to read it this time—just shook her head, wondering what the janitor was using to remove the stains each night.

Now that she lived nearer the office, she enjoyed the pleasure of having the condo to herself for the lunch hour. She would putter, read a book, water plants while she ate a sandwich. Sometimes she even remembered to take out meat to thaw for supper. Why, she asked herself, did this hour seem so enjoyable when the weekends without Megan or her work seemed too quiet and overlong?

As she left the main door of her building, she could hear sirens. Not unusual near the city centre. She walked slowly back to work, but when she was still a block away, two police cars raced past her. They pulled to a stop in front of her office, where several other police cars were already parked haphazardly.

She began to run. An ambulance was waiting at the building entrance, its red lights flashing and the doors wide open. Two attendants were carrying a stretcher carefully down the front steps, while a third walked alongside the patient, adjusting the medical equipment. Police were everywhere, speaking into their walkie-talkies.

"What's happened?" Lexie called out. Several social workers stood in the road, talking with the officers. But Dory Robertson was at the top of the steps, alone. She looked pale and diminished. Her hair was blowing in the cold March wind, and she had not even put on a jacket.

Lexie approached the stretcher. She recognized Janelle, her head swathed in bandages and her face white, bloodless. Her eyes were shut. Lexie stepped back, in shock.

She turned to Joan, "What's going on?"

"It was Sally. Sally did it. Oh, Jesus!"

"How? What did she do?"

But Joan was watching the attendants load Janelle into the ambulance. Dory suddenly rushed down to insist on going with her.

Joan grasped her arm. "I'll go with Janelle. You stay here." She gently pushed Dory toward the office door. "The police need to talk to you. I'll phone as soon as I know anything." As she climbed into the back of the ambulance, she called to Lexie, "Look after Dory. Get Bill to take her home when the police are finished with her."

"Bill." Lexie touched the other social worker on his sleeve. "What happened?"

He finally looked down at her. "Sally hid in the women's washroom. Stood on the toilet seat, apparently. Janelle was facing the mirror combing her hair when Sally burst out of the stall with a big knife."

"Oh, no!" Lexie cried. But Bill kept on talking, hardly noticing.

"Stabbed Janelle in the head. In the neck, too … I don't know how many times." He sighed raggedly. "God, I hope she doesn't die."

It was unbelievable. Lexie fought down nausea. The crowd watched silently as the ambulance pulled out. Then the staff turned and headed into the building. Blood was splattered in front of the elevator and inside it on the walls and floor. No one spoke. When they stepped out onto the third floor, there was blood everywhere. Some people murmured in dismay. Dory wept quietly. Bill pulled off his glasses, wiping away his tears with the back of his hand. Lexie pressed her lips together and held her breath as long as she could against the smell of the blood, unaware that she was massaging her stomach to ease the nausea.

The blood got under their shoes as they walked toward the office. It was on the walls. It was even on the ceiling above them. How could Janelle live without all this blood? The bathroom had been cordoned off, and police were inside.

Near the back of the hall, which led to a rear exit, Sally March sat on the floor, her legs splayed out in front of her. A police officer squatted next to her, holding a set of handcuffs. Sally was examining her bloodied hands, keening and crying out between her wails, "Sorry … sorry … sorry …"

The social workers moved into the reception area, where there was no blood. After being stabbed in the washroom, Janelle had run straight down the hall to the elevator, screaming for help. Now they found themselves taking seats in the waiting area, shaking their heads in disbelief, wiping their eyes, breathing in the cleaner air.

Lexie took a few deep breaths. "We'll need to close the office for a while … at least until everything is cleaned up and we hear how Janelle is," she pointed out. She picked up a sheet of paper and printed in large letters: MINISTRY OFFICE CLOSED UNTIL 3:00 P.M. She added the usual phone number for emergencies. Then she re-entered the main hall. Sally was gone. Walking gingerly to the elevator to avoid the blood, she rode down to the main entrance and taped the makeshift notice on the front door. On her way back, she watched several maintenance people cleaning the floors and walls. One was atop a high stepladder, working on the ceiling.

Back in the reception area, Bill was talking on the telephone to Joan. "Well, keep us posted," he said. Then he hung up and turned to the others. "It looks like Janelle will make it." There was a murmur of relief. "She's got eight stab wounds to the head—"

"That explains the blood spurting right up to the ceiling."

"—but none on her face," Bill continued. "She was stabbed three times in the neck. Just missed hitting the jugular."

"I can't believe it. I can't believe Sally would do that, she's never been violent before…. It must have been the apprehension of her daughter against her will." whispered Dory.

"We all missed on that, Dory. Not just you."

"She's only the receptionist, for God's sake. An innocent bystander," said Bill.

Then, seeking privacy, they shut the reception door and retreated to their offices. Lexie felt numb. *If I had stayed at work over the noon hour, it could have been me.* Then she felt ashamed that relief for her own safety was one of her first reactions.

Before the office reopened several hours later, the social workers sought each other out one by one, and tentative conversations began.

"Janelle's supposed to get married in six weeks."

"I guess the big wedding will be postponed now. Poor kid."

"Has anyone called her family? Her fiancé?"

"Dory gave the police their phone numbers."

"Where is Dory?"

"Bill took her home. She's pretty shook up."

"They had to shave Janelle's head. All that beautiful long black hair."

"That's the least of it—she could have been killed."

"Yeah, she'll have to get a wig."

"Dory feels terrible. It was Dory she was mad at."

"Why didn't one of us call the police about Sally before this happened? We knew who was doing the writing."

"Yeah. Hell, you know how it is. We get threatened all the time."

"Still, we should be calling the police more often. Look at that guy Sam. He's threatened to climb on top of the building across the street and pick us off with his rifle as we come out. Has anyone reported him?"

"I doubt it."

"It's still unbelievable," mused Lexie. "We've all learned how to be safe on home visits, at least as much as we can be. Keep the car keys handy, always take the chair closest to the door, never do an interview in the kitchen—too many knives around." She stopped and shivered.

After work, she hurried to pick up Megan. She stopped at the door and peered through the window until she spotted her daughter. She was lying on her stomach on the floor, paging through a colourful picture book, idly waving one of her sock-clad feet in the air, tranquil and contented.

Lexie swallowed as she realized—and the knowledge pierced her heart—how near the edge of disaster each of us live, unaware or simply choosing not to think about it. In seconds—the blink of an eye—one's whole life could be altered.

INTERVIEW WITH NORAH

NORAH SAT ON THE LIVING ROOM COUCH, CLAD IN A FLOWERED t-shirt and the new pale blue shorts she had insisted on wearing. She had one leg pulled up underneath her, and the other was stretched straight out, ending in a white sock and blue canvas runner that matched her shorts. Dodie had tied her long blonde hair into a ponytail with a blue elastic, and Lexie could see her pink scalp along the part line. Small boned and underweight, the child looked younger than her seven years.

For the first few minutes, Norah didn't look at Lexie. Instead she carefully examined her fingernails and modestly adjusted her shorts. Lexie gave her this time and then spoke quietly, introducing herself. "I'm a social worker, Norah. Do you know what that is?"

Norah raised her head, and Lexie was startled by her sudden piercing eye contact. "Last night, another social worker—his name was George—came with the police after I called the Helpline for kids. George brought me here to Dodie's house. The police took my mom and Walt away."

"Who is Walt?"

"He's my mom's boyfriend, but I don't like him. He's mean to her." She said all this without hesitation, as if she had known Lexie a long time. "I'm scared of him when they get drunk." Her skin was pale and delicate, and Lexie noticed a blue vein running along her jaw line. She was a beautiful child.

"What happens when they get drunk?" Lexie asked.

"They fight a lot. They yell and scream … and sometimes he hits her." Norah's composure was frightening.

"What happens to *you* when they are drunk?"

"I hide in my room."

"Then what happens?"

Norah thought about this for a few seconds, gazing upward and giving the question grave consideration. Her face closed over some memory, and she responded diffidently, looking away. "Nothing much. I fall asleep."

Lexie paused for a moment. *There's more here. Don't push her. I'm like a dentist, probing in anticipation of a painful but necessary extraction.* "I think I understand, but I'm not sure. Can you tell me more about some of the things that happen in your house?"

Norah shifted and straightened both legs in front of her. Her feet did not reach the floor. She primly adjusted the hem of her shorts again. "Well, I don't like it when my mom gets drunk and there's no food." She paused and looked across at Lexie, who nodded, waiting for more. "And I don't like it when she doesn't come home and I'm all alone. I get scared at night." Norah pursed her lips.

Go slowly now … she's trying to decide how much to tell me.

"And I don't like it if I come home from school and she's not there, and I have to stay outside."

"Is there any place you can go to when that happens?"

"No. We just moved here, and we don't know anybody.… And, anyway, my mom says not to talk to the neighbours."

"Last night the police took Walt to jail," Lexie explained, "but not your mom. They took her to the hospital because Walt had hurt her. She's feeling better now—I visited her just before I came here. I think she'll have to stay there a few more days, though."

"She's mad at me for calling the Helpline. She yelled at me. Walt says it's all my fault."

"That's not true, Norah. You did the right thing."

Without much conviction, the child tried to defend her mother. "Mom doesn't think so. She said if I told anybody, welfare would take me away."

"What happened isn't your fault."

"And you did, too." Norah was briefly defiant. "You're the welfare, aren't you?"

Lexie nodded again. "It wasn't safe for you there." She paused before she offered Norah a little bit of power. "What would you like to have happen now?"

The young girl thought for a moment. "I want my mom to stop drinking. I want her to find a nicer boyfriend." She continued in a half whisper. "He broke a bottle over her head, and before that he stuck a needle in her. He puts needles in their arms all the time." She sighed, then pointed out, "It's drugs, you know," as if she was afraid Lexie wouldn't understand.

Lexie exhaled softly as Norah gazed at her without blinking. She knew that Norah was trusting her with secrets and hoping that she would handle them carefully.

Norah finally blinked, looked down, and sighed as well. "Do you think she'll ever stop drinking? She stopped one time...." Her voice trailed off.

Lexie nodded in acceptance of Norah's pain. She would have loved to promise Norah that everything would turn out right, but she could not make easy assurances. And Norah was much too worldly to find comfort in gentle lies. "I've told your mom that you have to stay here with Dodie for a while. I'll help her, and other people will help her, too." Lexie paused. "Do you think you'll be okay here?"

"Dodie let me read to her." She smoothed out her shorts again. "And we went shopping for new clothes for me this morning."

"I see that.... I love the colour of your runners."

Norah's voice became husky, but she managed not to cry. "Can I see my mom?"

"As soon as she's out of hospital, I'll arrange for you to see her. But, Norah, I think the only way your mom can stop drinking and taking drugs is if she goes to a special treatment centre for a couple of months. You couldn't visit her there, but you could talk on the phone every day. And sometimes she can come here."

"If she isn't still mad at me."

"I don't think she'll be mad at you. I think she might be mad at herself, though, because she's not being a good mother to you right now, even though she loves you." Again she reassured Norah. "What happened is not your fault." They fell silent, and Lexie steeled herself for the next probe she must launch. "I see you have bruises between your legs, Norah. I think you need to tell me about that."

Norah shifted her weight and pulled at the legs of her shorts, another attempt to cover the deep purple marks. "They said not to tell."

"Who said not to tell?"

"Mom and Walt," she whispered.

"It's okay to tell, now."

"Walt hurt me in here." She pointed to her vagina and then looked up at Lexie. Her blue eyes were outraged, unable to comprehend why Walt would have done this to her.

"I know this is hard to talk about." Lexie inhaled deeply, repressing her sudden, murderous rage toward Walt and Norah's mother. "Thank you for trusting me." She resisted her impulse to reach across and gather Norah tightly in her arms. She knew that this little girl couldn't bear to be touched right then.

"But Mom will be mad." Now Norah was crying. "That's why they were fighting. She told him not to do that to me again, or she'd call the cops. She grabbed the butcher knife." Norah rubbed the tears off her cheeks. "He took it away from her and cut her on her cheek, and then he hit her lots of times." She shrugged in resignation. "He didn't have to do that. She wouldn't really phone the police."

God, when you can't even count on your own mother to protect you. "I'm so sorry all this happened to you." She gave Norah a moment to compose herself and then spoke again. "Norah, you and I have to go to the Children's Hospital now. I'll ask a doctor to check you and make sure you're okay. After that, a lady police officer will ask you to tell her exactly how Walt hurt you. If you can tell her about it, then it will help make sure that he doesn't hurt other children, too." Norah was trembling. As Lexie watched this frightened child, her own throat thickened. "I know it will be hard, but we need to do this."

Norah nodded slowly. "Can I come back here after?"

"Oh, yes. And then in a few days, we'll visit your mom, if you want."

"Yes." Norah adjusted her shorts again. "There's other kids living here. Did you take them from their moms, too?"

"Another social worker did."

"They're okay. But Kyle still wears diapers, and he's five years old."

"He's had a hard time."

"Yeah."

"It will get better. You're being very brave."

"Dodie and I made cookies. Would you like one?"

"I'd love that.... Thank you, Norah."

Norah jumped off the couch and went to the kitchen, where Dodie was waiting. Lexie made a note in her logbook and shook her head. It never got any easier, nor did her helpless rage at this particular crime lessen. She picked up her cell phone and called the sexual assault team at the Children's Hospital to confirm Norah's appointment. They told her a police officer was already standing by.

SECOND CHANCES

WHEN MEGAN WAS TWENTY-FOUR AND HAD COMPLETED HER degree in library sciences, she harnessed her self-confidence and—in Lexie's unbiased opinion—numerous skills and moved to New York City. Eventually Megan and her new husband, Ray, moved into a small apartment in Brooklyn.

With her daughter's apparently permanent residence in New York, Lexie determined to make an adventurous move of her own, one that would place her closer to Megan, yet still be respectful of her privacy. She had no difficulty obtaining a position in Halifax, where she rediscovered her love for the Maritimes. A year later, she remarried. Her new husband, Andy Wilcox, was a comfortable, gentle man, complete in himself, who made her happy.

One day at a foster home, she sat silently observing her new client, Abigail. Her mind sifted through the information Abigail's therapist, Kate, had given her in an earlier meeting. The therapist had cautioned, "Whatever you do, don't force her. Let her tell us when she's ready." Kate had paused and then added, "You can't send her back north. She needs counselling—and she needs to feel safe. We've established a rapport, and she's beginning to trust me. If she's sent back, that's just one more betrayal." Lexie nodded and smiled inwardly at being told how to behave after all these years she'd been in the field—not that it ever hurt to be reminded, she told herself.

Now Abigail was curled up in a big leather recliner, dressed in so many layers of clothes that she looked much heavier than she really was. At twelve, she was a beautiful girl with long, coarse, jet-black hair, a golden brown complexion, rosy cheeks covering high cheekbones, and rosebud lips. But her dark brown eyes, hidden by long lashes until she finally looked directly at Lexie, were those of someone in shock, someone who had been terrorized too long. They were the eyes of a fragile, angry survivor. She glared at Lexie, curled her lips in a sneer, and challenged every statement she made.

"Are you like my last social worker?" Abigail demanded.

"I don't know," Lexie replied. "What was she like?"

"I hate her.... I almost beat her up once." She stared defiantly at Lexie and then, turning her head away, went on. "I hated the one before her, too."

Lexie didn't react because she knew Abigail had never hit a social worker, although she had probably *wanted* to do it. She watched the girl a moment before she spoke again, "Do you hurt people very often?"

Abigail toyed with the fringe of the afghan she had pulled up to her chin to hide herself even more. "Just people who are mean to me."

Lexie kept silent.

"My mother was mean to me. Used to swear at me and hit me all the time. So did Gordon and Carolina—they used to beat on me every chance they got … Tom, too," she added with revulsion, her voice catching when she used her stepfather's name.

"Those are your older brother and sister, and your stepfather, right?"

"I hate them all."

"I guess that's why you came into care—because you weren't safe at home."

Abigail stood suddenly and moved toward Lexie, who sat opposite her on the couch. She leaned down until her face was inches from Lexie's. "I want to go home. Back to White Rapids," she screamed, then turned and slumped back into her chair.

Lexie waited a moment. "You haven't mentioned your other brother, Abigail…. You have a baby brother, don't you?"

"Duh! Why do you think I want to go home?" The girl shook her head in exasperation. "I'm the only one who looks after him, that's why."

Lexie was stunned. Tenderness and admiration surged through her. Abigail had been starved, beaten, taunted for her developmental delays, locked up in dark rooms, and raped repeatedly in that home, yet she was willing to endure it all again so she could look after her young brother. She still had the capacity to love.

"But Wilfred's safe now. He's in a foster home, too," Lexie pointed out.

"Yeah, I know," replied Abigail, still indignant. "But he gets to go home for visits. Stays overnight, too." Her face showed her inward struggle to articulate her thoughts. "I need to be there at night—when they party." Sorrowfully she added, "And to make sure he gets fed."

*   *

Though it was forbidden to take any files from the office, Lexie carted all six of Abigail's home that evening, marvelling at how information on a girl of just twelve could take up so many thick files. As she parked in her driveway that late afternoon, Andy was waiting for her, looking upset. He waved a slip of paper toward her. Lexie rushed out of the car. "What is it? Is it Megan?"

"Yes, Ray just phoned. She started her labour, and he's taking her to the hospital."

Her daughter, about to have a baby, and miles and miles away in New York City! She tore the note from Andy's hand and plumped down into the closest kitchen chair. All he had scrawled was, "Ray—Megan, hospital."

"When—when did he phone? Will he keep us updated?"

Andy took a chair across from her. "He says he'll call as soon as there's any news."

"What about the contractions? Did he say how far apart they were?"

Andy shrugged. "He was so excited … and I didn't think to ask."

Lexie shook her head in frustration. *Men!* But when she noticed how upset Andy looked, she reached across to pat his hand. She realized that her own hand was shaking. "He'll call as soon as he can. She's healthy—the baby, too," she said, both to comfort Andy and to reassure herself. Andy had only met Megan and her husband once. Since he had no children from his first marriage, he was feeling his way through the whole business now—stepdaughter, son-in-law, imminent birth of a grandchild.

"I made supper … just a light one," he offered. She smiled at him. They had been lucky to find each another—both had given up on new partnerships long before mutual friends had introduced them.

"I just have to get some work I brought home from the car. I got a real stinker of a new case today." Muttering to herself, she added, "As if I don't have a big enough caseload already." Andy shook his head. He always told her to leave her work at the office. Lexie seldom talked about her job—how could she, it was confidential—but she still struggled against bringing work home after she remarried. It had become a habit in her years of single parenthood—a way to keep up with ever-increasing bureaucracy and to fill in the hours once her daughter was asleep.

That evening, she alternated between pacing the floor, willing the phone to ring, and pouring through Abigail's files, which she had spread across the kitchen table. The girl was from northern Labrador, brought to Halifax by her foster mother, Tannis Ross, who had known Abigail since her birth. By interprovincial agreement, Nova Scotia Social Services supervised the case, but Newfoundland paid the bills. And, as Lexie scanned the first file, she realized just how huge those bills were. Cleaning services for the damage to Tannis's home when Abigail flew into a rage and for the extra work when she soiled the bed, which happened often, though medical examination showed no physical cause for it. Twenty hours of child support services per week. Two hours a week for therapy with Kate. And the payment to the foster mother, the highest on the scale. She remembered her supervisor, Merv, remarking, "It looks like she'll be here until she reaches majority. There just aren't the services up north that the girl needs—or relatives that can cope with her and keep her safe from her family…. She seems to have been the family scapegoat."

Lexie rested her head on the table, unable to stay focussed on her case. She pictured Megan in a maternity suite in some nameless hospital on Long Island, and, in sympathy, she *felt* her daughter's contractions. She walked to the front room window to stare out into the dark night, the phone in her hand. Then, back at the kitchen table, she paged through the health sections in Abigail's files. The various diagnoses from doctors, mental health workers, and school psychologists confirmed what she had seen and heard from Kate, and from Abigail herself. The girl tested in the seventies for IQ—though environmental factors affected this quotient. She suffered from post-traumatic stress disorder and ADD, and was oppositional-defiant. Lexie wondered at the accuracy of all the diagnoses accumulated over the years. In any case, it would be a long, slow process to heal this girl. Although she had recovered from the final assault that had caused multiple fractures and led to an emergency airlift to St. John's for treatment, the emotional impact of years of abuse might not be overcome. And now Abigail had been moved to a completely alien world. How would she cope?

Andy finally went to bed at midnight. Lexie knew he did not expect her to join him soon. He knew she'd stay awake—for days if necessary—until that phone rang. *Let them both be okay, let them both be okay*, she willed silently. She tried again to focus on the files before her. She discovered that Abigail's mother had shown up at a prenatal clinic only once, very drunk, and had staggered drunk into the same clinic to give birth. "Poor kid," Lexie muttered. "She's probably got Fetal Alcohol Syndrome as well as everything else."

As soon as Lexie's own daughter had suspected she was pregnant, she had given up coffee, soft drinks, and tea. Shyly, she told her mother that she had wanted a baby for as long as she could remember. Lexie knew Megan would be refusing all medications and pain blockers during this labour, fiercely determined to give birth as naturally as possible. And Ray would never leave her side, either. *But why, oh why, doesn't he phone?*

She bent over the files again. The RCMP, following the directions of the nearest social worker two hundred miles south, had apprehended Abigail when she was just shy of two weeks old. Her mother, drunk again, had stumbled and dropped her onto the floating dock on the shore of White Lake. She was arrested for public drunkenness and endangering the life of an infant. The doctor who had delivered Abigail such a short time before checked her over at the clinic and determined that the fall had not caused serious injury. Then he had taken her to the home of friends—the local mechanic and his wife, Tannis, who was a nurse. They fell in love with Abigail, and wanted to adopt her, but a month later she was returned to her birth mother. How different her life might have been, Lexie thought, had the social worker and the court shown foresight and courage before more damage was done. But the birth parent always gets more than one chance—if the kid's still alive. She wondered what torturous childhood had brought Abigail's mother to this state of degradation, unable to care, seeking oblivion.

Sometime after midnight, Lexie gathered Abigail's files and slipped a heavy elastic around them. She boiled the kettle for tea and began pacing, clutching the phone in her hand. She stared through the window at the stars overhead and prayed to an entity she was now fairly sure didn't exist. About an hour later, she felt herself calming down. She lay on the couch and fell asleep immediately. The phone, cradled against the curve of her stomach, woke her at 2:45. Immediately alert, she pushed the "on" button.

"Hi, Mom, it's me."

"Megan!"

"I told Ray to wait until I was back in my room because I wanted to talk to you first. Oh, Mom." She sounded tired but elated. "You have a beautiful granddaughter! She was born almost an hour ago—at 12:48 our time."

Lexie's eyes swelled with tears. "Oh, a girl." It was what she had secretly hoped for. "Tell me all about it."

It was only later, after she'd wakened Andy to tell him about the wonderful new baby, Amy Jane, that she recalled the sense of peace that had entered her just before she lay on the couch and fell deep into sleep—at about the time her granddaughter was born. She marvelled. Somehow she had known when the baby had been safely delivered, when all was well. The wonder of love.

• ◆ •

Abigail and Lexie met every two weeks for the next six months and slowly began to form a relationship. Abby was an extremely volatile child, and the only way Lexie could cope with her in public places was by remaining as calm as possible, no matter the provocation. And occasionally she was rewarded with Abby's trust, however fleeting.

While Lexie was striving to forge a bond with Abby, the foster mother and the teachers at the learning centre (a euphemism for the segregated classroom of developmentally delayed students) were struggling with Abby's toileting—in addition to her other behaviours.

She refused breakfast each day, unwillingly took a packed lunch to school, which she never ate, and rejected all liquids. It was clear she was doing this to avoid the humiliation of wetting or soiling herself. But it took a while for Tannis and staff to understand that Abby was also terrified to enter public bathrooms.

Tannis often updated Lexie by phone. When Abby first began living with her, it had taken weeks to get the child to use the bathroom at the new home in Halifax. At last, terrified, Abigail had agreed to enter the room only if Tannis sat outside the door and maintained a steady conversation with her. It took even more time to coax Abby to have a shower—to do more than turn the faucet on, watch the water flow down the drain, and emerge from the bathroom swearing that she'd washed, used soap, and shampooed her hair, even though it was clear she had neither disrobed nor gotten more than one hand wet. But Tannis had persisted. Although it was two steps forward and one step back, and Abigail never lost her fear of the bathroom, she did actually begin to use the toilet most of the time and to bathe more often than not. But the foster mother had to stay just outside the door each time.

On the tried and true theory that children relax their barriers more easily over food—avoiding eye contact by picking at their hamburgers or pouring huge dollops of ketchup over the French fries—Lexie often took the kids on her caseload out for lunch or for snacks after school. Abby seemed thrilled at the idea of going to a restaurant, but Lexie worried that this might be the wrong thing to do with this particular child.

When Lexie arrived to pick her up, Abby had managed to hide herself at the back of the classroom, behind a movable blackboard. Was she preparing herself for disappointment should Lexie forget to come? Or was she fearful of the public experience ahead of her? But the teachers privately told Lexie that Abby had bragged to the other children about her social worker and her lunch date, and had spent the morning anxiously looking out the window in wait. Why then did she leave the classroom so reluctantly, and why did she make such a big point of ignoring Lexie altogether?

Yet once in the car, she began talking quite normally—for Abby—demanding this, wanting that, challenging Lexie. "Why are you making me stay in that lousy foster home? Why can't I go home? Why do you come to see me, anyway?" Then she added a new question. "Why do you want to have lunch with me today?" Lexie always answered the questions the same way. It had become a mantra. "It's a good home for you." "Tannis likes having you live with her." "You can't go home because it's not safe for you there." "I come to see you to make sure you're still safe and because I like you." This time she added an answer to Abigail's new question. "I want to have lunch with you so we have a chance to talk and get to know each other better." Abby never questioned these responses. They seemed to soothe her.

The lunch was tense. Abby couldn't read the menu and threw it aside in disgust, shouting, "I'm not even fuckin' hungry." The waitress watched them out of the corner of her eye. Lexie silently picked up the menu from the floor and spoke quietly, "Hmmm … it says they have fish and chips … hamburgers … sandwiches … I think I'll have a bacon and tomato sandwich. Would you like one?" She did not mention that Tannis had told her this was Abby's favourite food.

"Does it come toasted?" Abby asked suspiciously.

"Let me see … yes, on white or brown bread."

"I want white bread, but not burnt!"

When the lunch came, Abby watched curiously as Lexie picked up half a sandwich and took a bite.

"Is it any good?" she asked doubtfully.

"Mmmm … it's delicious."

Carefully, as if it might be poisonous, Abigail picked up her sandwich, sniffed it, and gingerly took a bite. Lexie carried on eating, pretending not to notice. One bite seemed to satisfy Abby that the food was edible and not too scary. She ate the entire sandwich and then tried the coleslaw. Her face twisted in horror. She opened her mouth and let the food fall to the plate. "Ugh," she screamed, "that's terrible!" She grabbed her glass of root beer and swigged it down to wash away the taste.

"You don't like cabbage salad?" asked Lexie, as calmly as she could, her appetite gone at the sight of partly chewed food and saliva dripping down Abby's chin and onto her plate.

She handed Abigail a napkin. Then she picked up her own, wiped her mouth, and said, casually, "I have to go to the bathroom now. See, it's right over there." She pointed across the room. "Will you be okay here, or do you want to come with me?" She watched in silence as the conflict played across Abigail's face. Which was more terrifying: sitting alone at the table or going into that public bathroom? Lexie was flooded with guilt. Why was she compelling the child to make this double-edged choice? Did she really think this would build up Abigail's trust in her?

"I guess I'll go with you," Abby finally muttered. Reluctantly she followed Lexie across the room.

In the washroom, Abigail assumed her usual stance: legs slightly spread for better balance, arms stiffly at her side, hands in fists, ready for anything. Lexie pointed to a stall and said, "I'll just go in here." She chatted steadily through the closed door. "I'm glad there's nobody else here but you. I hate using a toilet when there's a bunch of strangers around." She flushed the toilet and exited the stall. "Say, do you want to pee while I wash my hands? I'll be right here."

Abigail struggled. She closed her mouth, then opened her mouth; clenched and unclenched her fists. Finally she answered, "Might as well, I guess. Too many kids at school."

As Lexie listened to Abby empty her swollen bladder, it felt like a major victory.

* ◆ *

"I'm going away for two weeks." Lexie tentatively began.

"Two weeks!" Abigail shrieked. She turned her head away, stared out the window on the passenger side of the car, and began drumming her feet anxiously on the floor. "Why are you going away?" Her voice trembled. She thumped the window with her right hand, embarrassed by her own emotion.

"I have to see some people, but I'll come back."

"Oh, *sure*. Everybody says that—but they don't." She plucked at a food stain on her oversized sweatshirt.

Lexie drew her appointment book out of her purse and took hold of the pen attached to it. "We'll set a date right now for our next meeting." She paged through the dates. "I'll be back on the sixth, so we can meet on the ninth. I'll pick you up at school at eleven-thirty, the same as always." She filled out a card and handed it to Abby, who read it carefully, lips moving with the effort, and jammed it into her pocket.

"Why can't we meet on the sixth? You're back then."

"Because I have to catch up at the office before I can go out to see you and the other kids I meet with."

"I want to phone my mom. Right now." This apparent change of subject was typical of Abby. But Lexie understood the connection: "Mom" was another person who had abandoned her, who would disappear for days and weeks at a time.

Tannis was uncomfortable allowing the girl to phone her relatives back home because, as she had pointed out, "She's always upset after she talks to them. They make promises that they never keep." But Lexie had decided that Abby needed to make these calls to her family, even if they only reinforced the disappointing and painful connection. So she took her to the office once a month to use the phone. "Well," she answered Abigail now, "you phoned them just two weeks ago, but I guess we can put in an extra call this one time."

Lexie always stayed in the office when Abby phoned, and the girl never questioned this lack of privacy. Once, after Lexie had listened to the first few calls, she decided that she didn't need to be present and had picked up her files to work temporarily down the hall in another room. But Abby had called her back. "Hey, where are you going? Stay here!" she had ordered, glaring at Lexie and frantically pointing to the empty chair. Lexie had been surprised at first, but Abby needed her as a safety net in case the call was a bad one—if her mother was drunk or if hasty, insubstantial promises were made yet again.

Today's phone call was innocuous. Abby burbled away to an unresponsive, uninterested brother and then asked to speak to her mother. But she was away, no one quite knew where. Abby seemed satisfied when she hung up—she had made contact, she had offered her love—*she* was not the one who was abandoning her family.

It always made Lexie's heart ache when this happened, when Abby hung up the phone, turned to her, and said, "Mom's away," or "Gordon's in jail again," or "Caroline says she's going to come here next month and visit me!" inevitably followed up two weeks later with, "She can't come down after all. No money."

Lexie often had to remind Abby that broken promises weren't necessarily lies. "People," she had explained gently, "often say they'll do things for you, or buy things for you, when they can't. I think they say these things because they *wish* it could happen that way."

• ◆ •

Lexie flew to New York the next morning and took a cab from Kennedy Airport to Ray and Megan's apartment in Brooklyn. Ray was waiting in front of the brownstone, and after they greeted and hugged each another, he pointed up to the living room window of the apartment on the second floor. There stood Megan, waving at her and holding Amy Jane. A great relief swept through Lexie. They really were okay.

For the next two weeks, she immersed herself in the joy of her perfect granddaughter and the deep contentment of being with her only child, whose heart seemed to be connected to hers by a long, elastic, bungee-like cord. It could stretch to cover thousands of miles and months of time, yet coiled back, relaxed and inert, when they were together. She got to know Ray better this time, and she would never forget opening her eyes early one morning, from her place on the pull-out couch in the living room, to see Ray gently carrying his newborn daughter to the coffee table, where he adroitly changed her diaper while Megan lay asleep in the apartment's only bedroom.

Lexie and Andy's gift had been a wonderful English-style pram, and she took photo after photo of Megan and Ray pushing it, with Amy Jane sleeping contentedly inside, as they strolled through Central Park in Manhattan one Sunday afternoon.

She did not think about Abigail—or Dion or Michelle or Rhonda or Kevin or any other of the children on her caseload—until the two weeks were nearly over. It was only as she was packing and checking over her return flight ticket that they began to intrude into her mind. When she was nearly ready to go, Megan and Ray asked her to stay longer, to change her ticket. "You're here at just the right time, Mom. Ray could only be at home with Amy and me for two weeks." Megan stopped, her eyes shiny with tears. "He has to work through the night so often." Ray was working for HBO and had only the nights to edit the days' takes. In addition to that, he was working on a children's Christmas movie in the afternoons. They would desperately need this extra money to cover themselves when Megan's maternity leave benefits ran out in two months. Mornings were his only time to sleep.

Lexie was torn. Her own child came first, and her new grand-daughter. How could she abandon them? But they had Ray, and Megan was a grown, competent woman. Lexie had made promises to the children on her caseload. *Someone else can see them. You're completely replaceable. Don't ever forget it,* she told herself, but she also knew that realistically, unless there was a huge emergency, nobody would see them. The other social workers had their own demands to meet. She lay awake that night seeing faces of the children and of her daughter.

At the airport the next day, before she flew back to Andy and her caseload, she phoned Megan. They both cried, but assured each other that all would be well. Lexie couldn't bear to speak to anyone on the flight home. *We all fail our children in some way*, she thought regretfully, her hands clutched in fists.

* ◆ *

Tannis came into the office without an appointment the first day Lexie was back at work.

"You'll need to find another home for Abby," she announced. "I've had her a year now, and I love her dearly—you know that." She paused. "If only they'd let Ron and me keep her way back when Dr. McLeod brought her to us—instead of waiting until all the horrendous damage was done and I was a widow."

Lexie waited.

"But I'm getting older, and I can't do it any more." She proceeded to tell Lexie what kind of home Abigail needed.

"It may take some time," Lexie pointed out carefully. *As if I can just order up a home from the Sears catalogue*, she thought bitterly. She knew Tannis was tired—Abigail would surely exhaust many a foster parent—but this foster mother had done fantastic work with the child.

"Oh, I know, I know … I feel terrible about this," Tannis continued, "but if you could find a home soon, then we'd have a month to make the transition." Lexie didn't respond, and Tannis flushed. "I'm at the end of my rope," she confessed. "I don't expect you to do it tomorrow—and I don't want to lose contact with Abigail. Maybe I could move into a sort of grandmother role. You know, have her over for the weekend every once in a while?"

After Tannis left, Lexie considered what to do. Where on earth would she find foster parents who could cope with Abigail? She walked down to the resource worker's office. "I've got a problem, Mona," she began.

"Don't tell *me* about problems!" Mona exploded and her face flushed. "I've got to find a home for a sibling group of four. John's just removed them—they've only got the clothes on their backs, and they've all got lice." She was peering at her computer, scanning the short list of available homes, and picking up the phone all at the same time. "Everybody's full," she moaned. Lexie waved her hand. "I'll come back later, when you've sorted this out." Mona was dialing another number as she nodded her head.

Near the end of the day, she stopped by Lexie's office. When she learned that a new home was needed for Abigail, she swore and then mused thoughtfully, "What about the Morrises?"

"The Morrises?" questioned Lexie, and then she began thinking. "Alice is First Nations, isn't she?"

"Yeah, and they haven't had any placements for over a year. Still getting over Tiffany." Tiffany, the teenaged girl last placed in their home, had stolen from them, abused their young daughter, and told her girlfriends at the local high school that Jack and Alice were beating her all the time. She later admitted to Lexie that she had made it all up because she was furious at her foster parents for grounding her for a third time. But Tiffany's malicious remarks had gone well beyond her friends' ears; they had spread to the teachers and then out into the community. The Morrises and their children had been devastated.

"They're wonderful people," Lexie said thoughtfully. "Very calm and laid back." Then she smiled and shook her head slightly.

Mona smiled ruefully. "Yeah. I know, I know."

"Not exactly *Better Homes and Gardens*. But they are the kindest, most gentle people I know." Lexie was beginning to feel hopeful.

"And the mess is because they prioritize differently—children first, housework as there's time," Mona interrupted, always ready to support her foster homes to the death. "They might be just right for her."

"Do you think they'll be able to handle her? I'd hate for the placement to fall apart—and Abigail's a real challenge."

"There's no one else—and you know how skilled they are," Mona declared, exhausted and ready to go home.

Jack and Alice agreed to take the girl. Alice had cried when she heard some of the details of the girl's background—as much as Lexie was allowed to tell. It was time to tell Abigail.

Lexie was dreading it. How would the girl react to another rejection, another perceived betrayal? She brought Abigail into the office after school one afternoon and carefully began. "You've lived with Tannis a long time now."

Abby looked at her suspiciously. "Yeah, so what? Why are you saying that?" She glared across the room at Lexie, her eyes bright with unshed tears. "You're going to move me, aren't you?" She stood up, closing the distance between them. Then she bent over to face Lexie, only inches away. Her words, punctuated with sharp pauses, were spoken in a flat, unequivocal tone. "I—don't—want—to—move. Got that?" A silence fell, and Abigail flung herself defiantly back in her chair.

"Tannis thinks you'd do better with younger foster parents," Lexie began again, hastily adding, "She loves you very much and still wants you to visit her on some weekends, but she wants to be like a grandma to you instead of a foster mother."

"I've got a grandma. She's a drunk, too, just like my stupid mother."

Lexie sighed. "I am so sorry this is happening, Abigail. But, you know, Tannis would be a good grandmother. And in this other home, there is a brother and a sister, but you'd be the oldest. You'd be the big sister."

"I knew it wouldn't last." Abigail stared at Lexie hopelessly. "Nothing good ever does."

Lexie nodded gently, acknowledging Abby's disappointment. "I wish it wasn't that way for you, Abby." She waited a moment before speaking again. "But I would like you to meet Jack and Alice and the kids. They *want* you to live with them, and they're hoping you'll at least meet them and give them a chance."

Abigail nodded miserably. "When do I have to move?"

"Not for a while. You have to feel okay about your new home first. But before Christmas." It was mid-November.

Lexie planned the transition to Alice and Jack Morris's home very carefully. She involved Tannis from the beginning, asking that she and Alice arrange several short visits to the Morrises for Abigail in the first week, followed by a weekend visit without an overnight stay. Both foster mothers reported that the meetings were positive. Now only three weeks of transition were left, and it was time to prepare Abigail for an overnight visit. By now Alice had a good understanding of Abby's toileting and hygiene issues, and Lexie felt sure she would be sensitive to them. But did Abigail feel safe enough at the Morrises to spend the night without Tannis for support?

Lexie met with Abigail alone, picking her up over the noon hour as usual. She assured the girl that these lunches would not change. Initially the meeting started as all meetings with Abigail began. She climbed into the car and immediately harangued Lexie about school, about her foster mother, and now about her future foster mother. She always ended her tirade in the same way. "Why do I have to have *you* as my social worker? There must be somebody better over in that big, stupid office!"

Lexie let a silence fall before responding in her usual way. She waited to see if Abigail was ready to talk about what was really bothering her. As Lexie was backing out of the school parking lot, Abby spoke again.

"That Alice is a good cook.... But her kids are sure brats."

Lexie laughed. "Little kids can be pests, all right, but Alice told me they really like you. They're pestering her all the time about when you're coming to see them again."

"Little pests, that's what they are for sure." But Abby's voice had softened, and she smiled at the thought of the two children. "They climb all over me. They never leave me alone." It was then that Lexie realized Abby only allowed physical contact with children.

"What about Jack? Have you talked with him much?"

"He's crazy!" Abby laughed again at some memory. "We went tobogganing, and he kept pushing us off. Me and Sharon and Jason were always in the snowdrifts!"

Unbelievable! She even likes Jack—a man. Oh, this is too good to be true.

Over lunch at McDonald's—Abigail's favourite restaurant—Lexie was regaled with a long, detailed account of the toboggan expedition, and of baking cookies with Jack, going for a walk with Alice, and watching videos with the children.

"Alice won't let me swear." Abigail sent Lexie a piercing glare.

"How does she stop you?"

"Oh, she just gets this sad look and says nobody swears in their house. She's religious, I think."

"How do you feel about that?"

"I try not to swear. It's not good in front of little kids—even if they *are* terrible brats."

Lexie laughed, and after a moment, so did Abby.

"Alice phoned me to come over for the weekend.... What do you think?" Abigail sounded doubtful.

"She phoned me, too," Lexie responded. They were silent for a moment. "I could drive you over on Friday after school, and Alice and Jack will take you back to Tannis on Sunday afternoon."

Abigail looked down at her lap, worried.

"Tannis says she'll phone you every night, and she'll come and get you if you're not comfortable there."

When lunch was over, Lexie drove Abby back to school. She pulled into the schoolyard, found a parking spot, then shut off the engine and turned to Abigail. "I think you should give it a try." Abigail nodded slowly. Then she opened the car door and ran off toward the school without another word. Lexie watched her jerk open the door and slam it shut. *How does that girl manage to slam a door that works on hydraulic pressure? And why is she running off? Does she not want to admit that it might be okay? Or does she feel pushed? Does she think that I'm not aware of her fears?*

●—◆—●

On December 22, the beginning of the school Christmas break, Abigail officially moved into the Morris foster home, after having spent the last three weekends there. It looked like the placement was going to work, and Lexie felt good. Until Alice phoned her one morning.

"How's it going?" Lexie asked.

"Oh, good," Alice responded. "She's fitting in real good. The kids just love her, as you know." But something was bothering Alice, and Lexie waited patiently for her to get around to the issue. "It's Tannis," Alice finally and hesitantly revealed. "She's a very nice person, and she took good care of Abby." She paused again. Complaining was not in her nature. "But now I'm Abby's foster mother, and it's very confusing for her. Tannis phones every day. She questions me, then she questions Abigail, then she gets me on the phone again and tells me what I should be doing." Alice sounded completely frustrated.

"I'll call her. I'm sure she's having a hard time right now. Letting go may not be as easy as she thought it would be."

But when Lexie telephoned, Tannis got angry. "First you want me involved, and now you want me to back off. *I'm* the one who drove Abby back and forth to the Morrises and spent hours there just sitting around. All for Abigail. *I'm* the one who worried about her on those overnight visits." Before Lexie could reply, Tannis continued, her voice rising in passion. "*I'm* the one that knows her best! I'm the one that loves her...."

Oh boy, Lexie sighed. *Nothing is ever easy.*

Lexie organized a meeting, and Alice and Jack brought Abigail to the office. Kate and Tannis attended as well. They began to talk about roles, but Tannis interrupted when she spotted a tensor bandage around Abigail's knee. "What *happened* to you?" she asked.

"Oh, I hurt myself on the toboggan."

"Have you seen a doctor?"

Alice's usually placid face reddened. "Yes, I took her to the clinic and they x-rayed it. It's nothing to worry about."

But Tannis was oblivious to Alice's anger. "Let me see." She reached over to examine the bandage. "That doesn't protect it much."

Abigail rubbed her knee thoughtfully.

Lexie placed her hand lightly on Tannis's shoulder. "I'm sure it's okay."

"It's the bandage the doctor put on." Alice was seething.

"Maybe the play is too rough on the toboggan," retorted Tannis.

Kate picked up on the issue, and by the end of the meeting, Lexie was hopeful that it might be resolved. Tannis reluctantly agreed to cease her daily telephone calls to Abigail and to let the new foster parents make the parenting decisions. It was hard for her, Lexie could see. Tannis felt guilty about having the child moved and was greatly attached to her. Rationally, she understood what the social worker and counsellor were saying, but letting go emotionally would be much harder.

Abigail thrived and bloomed in her new placement. There were setbacks—she was sent home from school more than once for outbursts; her hygiene issues continued, especially during her menses; she ran away from home two or three times (never making it past the end of the block because of her fears), and she constantly griped about the Morris children. Yet Lexie noticed that Abby often begged to have them join her on their outings. She smiled to herself.

Alice took Lexie up north to visit her natural family. This was no easy journey—it involved buses, a ferry, truck rides, and a float plane.

They stayed in a band elder's home on the reserve, even though Abby nagged to stay at her mother's. Abby's stepfather had gone away for the duration of the visit—a condition Lexie had demanded—but Alice still guarded Abigail zealously during the three-day visit. Miraculously, she also seemed to gain the trust of Abby's mother.

As time went by, Tannis became more comfortable with her new role, and Abby regularly spent weekends at her home. She was successful as a grandmother figure and provided the Morrises with the break they sometimes needed.

Since the education system constantly needed to find new sources to fund Abigail's special needs, they looked for more labels. So Lexie began the process of having the girl tested at the Halifax Fetal Alcohol Syndrome Centre. It took several months for all the forms to be completed, but at last an appointment was arranged.

Abigail and Alice met Lexie at the centre. Abigail was already in a state of high apprehension—testing situations made her anxious. As she began to do a simple memory test, her behaviour became increasingly difficult to control. In a crescendo of frustration, she tore through the offices, knocking files off desks, erasing messages from a blackboard, flinging pens and pencils through the air, and slamming out the front door. Lexie, Alice, and the centre staff stood silently for a moment. Then Lexie went after the girl and found her huddled on the sidewalk, a few yards down the street. She crouched down beside Abby and waited silently.

"I hate that place!" the girl stormed. Her face was red, and she was panting with distress.

"I know," Lexie acknowledged.

"Do I have to go back there?"

"Alice is waiting for you, but we can stay out here for a little while." Abigail lifted her head and looked at Lexie, who gently smiled. "But I'm getting too old to squat like this, so let's walk around a bit."

Abby giggled. "You're not *that* old … but I'll walk with you if you want."

Later, Alice and Lexie watched through a one-way window as Abby struggled through a series of simple arithmetic skills questions. Once again her face was red, but she was visibly trying to control her frustration, her sheer rage at the situation that highlighted her inadequacies. Lexie watched tensely. Would she explode again? She glanced over at Abby's foster mother, standing quietly next to her. Tears were running down Alice's face as she watched her foster daughter suffer.

Oh, she loves that child. She really loves Abby. Lexie turned her head away in respect and awe. Alice loved Abby, a girl so many found completely unlovable. For a moment, she envied the woman's essential goodness, and then she was simply immensely grateful for it.

Months later, the test results came back confirming that Abby suffered from Fetal Alcohol Effect. The school was able to get the extra funding it needed for a teacher's aide for her. Lexie assured Abigail that she would never have to go back to the centre again. Abby was greatly relieved.

Lexie and Alice met once a month with Abby's therapist to discuss the girl's progress and to keep them all on track, each aware of the others' concerns and insights. At one of these meetings, they were discussing Abigail's adjustment to her new home.

"I'm really pleased," began Kate. "It's been difficult for her, processing Tannis's defection—and she's still dealing continually with her loyalty to her first family."

Alice and Lexie nodded.

"But she can never live there again. She's simply too vulnerable."

Alice spoke. "She said she never told anybody about what her stepfather was doing to her because he might get into trouble, and then her little brother wouldn't have a father any more." Alice looked off into space. "But she made me promise never to tell anyone … and here I am telling you."

Kate reassured her. "We're in this together. We all want to help Abby, and to do that, we need to know how she perceives her world." She sighed and straightened her back. "It's good that she's talking to you. You're the first person she's trusted with any information about the sexual abuse. She wouldn't even tell the police—they got the facts from witnesses."

Alice was still troubled. "She talks all the time about going back. Her sister had a baby, and Abby's determined to go up there and look after him. She doesn't trust her to look after the baby properly."

Lexie spoke up. "I haven't told Abby yet, but the baby's been taken into care. Her sister and her boyfriend were drunk last weekend, and they tried to canoe across the river with the baby. It was lucky they didn't all drown when the canoe overturned. There was a storm that night, but someone saw the canoe flip and was able to rescue them."

Kate shook her head. "But it's nearly winter!"

Alice nodded slowly. Then she asked, "What were they trying to do? Was it an emergency?"

"They were headed to town to buy more beer."

There was a moment of silence. They thought of the baby, of the sister lost in that soul-deadening world of drunkenness and squalor. What would become of Abby if she ended up back there?

Impulsively, Lexie turned to Alice. "You and Jack could adopt Abby." She hadn't even been aware that she was thinking of it.

Alice looked across the room at Lexie, and then down at her hands resting in her lap. "Yes," she said, "I think we must."

• ◆ •

Jack and Alice formally adopted Abigail three years after she had moved into their home. They knew that given Abby's childhood damage, her learning disabilities, and her Fetal Alcohol diagnosis, they had made a lifelong commitment. But now Abby had a permanent refuge—no matter what.

• ◆ •

Several years later, after she had retired from full-time work, Lexie was sitting in a coffee shop with a friend when Abigail strode by. She stopped short when she spied her old social worker. "Hi," she said.

"Abby! It's wonderful to see you…."

"I graduated from grade twelve. The first one in my family," Abigail proclaimed loudly as the coffee shop patrons turned to watch.

"I heard about that. I'm so proud of you."

Abigail reached out her hand tentatively and touched Lexie's shoulder. "You're the best social worker I ever had. You know that?"

Lexie looked into Abby's eyes. If it is true that the eyes can transmit a message, then Lexie was being enfolded lovingly in Abigail's arms.

FULL CIRCLE

LEXIE IS SIXTY. HER HAIR IS STILL RED—BRIGHTER THAN EVER
before, with the help of red rinses. She thinks of this as her only
vanity, although of course she is wrong. She has gained weight to
a uniform chubbiness—from plump cheeks to rolls around her
waist, a rounder bum to thickened thighs. Even her ankles and feet
are wider. She wears loose, casual clothing, which she chooses for
comfort and colour, not for style.

Except for the lingering hot flashes and sleeplessness, Lexie is
content. She is gradually accepting the loss of ecstasy in her life as
a fair exchange for a seasoned mind and the freedom to walk and
think on her own terms.

She is easier on herself, even though she knows less than she had
hoped she would by now. But this lack of knowledge is offset by
a greater understanding and tolerance, and an ability to recognize,
to predict, how things are likely to turn out. She has rediscovered
writing, something she used to do in her first years out of university.
She attends a weekly writing class and is often excited by her discov-

eries. Although she occasionally daydreams of another life—one in which her accomplishments are acknowledged with awards, money, and fame—she has reluctantly concluded that she is, after all, an ordinary woman.

Lexie and Andy have been married for years now. It is a loving relationship because they have both learned from painful past unions the importance of kindness.

She and Andy both work part time and enjoy a life that poses few hardships. Andy worked for years as a builder, the owner of a successful business. But with the move from Halifax to this coastal village thirty miles away, he has downsized to a small workshop attached to the back of their house. He does fine carpentry now, crafting wardrobes and coffee tables, which take him months to complete. He is building a wooden boat that Lexie is convinced will never be finished, and she interprets the project as an unconscious attempt at immortality.

As a grandmother, Lexie is beguiled, hopelessly in love with Amy Jane, who is utterly charming and intelligent. Once more, she has a child of her blood for whom she would wreak war to keep from harm. But for all her fierce feelings, she wryly accepts that she cannot entirely protect this small girl from the casual cruelties of life. As compensation, Lexie has no doubt that her own love, added to that of the child's parents, will give Amy the tools to wend her way.

Lexie continues in her profession of social work, still loving it and hating it. However, she has finally arrived at what she sees as the best this career can offer—a half-time caseload of seventeen teenagers, who have all, at different times in their lives, been made permanent wards of the province. Lexie is their delegated guardian. It is her job to help them prepare for adulthood and independence from the system in which they have been raised. For two and a half days each week, she drives to her office in Halifax, does the usual and ever-increasing administrative work, and visits her wards. Some are in foster homes, and some already live semi-independently in room-and-board situations. One of them is usually in jail. Another, named Shannon, disappears for weeks at a time, resurfacing only when she has run out of booze, drugs, and friends or if she is too sick to carry on.

Lexie is pretty clear about which of the seventeen teenagers will "make it" and which will likely spend a brutish lifetime in and out of bureaucratic systems, from welfare to transition houses, and from women's shelters to jail. She does her best for all of them, while aware that at this stage of their lives, she has limited impact. Each child has either incorporated enough strengths to thrive or has been too damaged to get by anywhere except on the unfriendly edges of society.

She tries sometimes to explain this to Andy, carrying on about the importance of early intervention. She decries the lack of courage in government policy, which plays only as far as the next election, or even more discouragingly, the next media poll. Andy watches her as she goes on. He is usually sanding something—the curve of a rocker or the rough planking for a table top—and his movements are steady and assured. He is careful not to interrupt, although he has heard these diatribes many times before. Sometimes he tells her she should quit. "We could go south for the winter." Or more cunningly, "You could see more of Amy."

But by the time Lexie has gone for a walk along the beach, prepared a light supper, or talked to Megan and Amy, who has not yet grasped that nodding into the telephone is not sufficient repartee, she has forgotten her anger and fatigue. "Two more years," she tells Andy. "This part time really is a cinch. Besides, I want to see what will happen to some of the kids—it's hard not to get attached, you know."

What frustrates her the most after years of social work is the cyclical nature of dysfunction and the natural process of recurrence. When she sees her client Shannon—the one who turns up every month or so and who, at fifteen, has progressed from marijuana to cocaine to crack—she talks with her about detox treatment, birth control, and counselling. Lexie becomes more and more urgent in pressing her. In fact, she wishes she could have her locked up long enough to detoxify her. She reminds Shannon that only a few years ago, the two of them attended the funeral of Shannon's own mother, who had died of a heroin overdose. *Why is Shannon going down the same dark road? How can I help her see that she is worth more, and can fairly expect more from life?* It tears her heart out to watch Shannon growing unhealthier from month to month before her eyes—her golden hair bleached and dry, her pale complexion mottled and pimpled, and her body becoming razor thin and bruised by needles, ravaged by the punishments of johns and her pimp.

There is no mistaking Shannon for what she has become. She has changed from a frightened young child to this tough street chick whose very stance confronts and intimidates ordinary citizens. When Lexie takes her for a meal now, she is aware that strangers glance surreptitiously, making their own guesses about the relationship between this middle-aged, conservatively dressed woman and the young, strung-out prostitute.

Lexie would like to hold Shannon, to take her back in time to her infancy and begin again. This time the child would never be left to cry for hours, to suck on sour milk from a dirty bottle, to be sworn at, shoved, pushed, slapped, kicked and then, bewilderingly, to be cuddled and cosseted by the same mother. If Lexie could grow Shannon again, she would fill her days with gentleness and consistency, and with boundaries that made her feel safe, cherished, and worthy.

Even now, despite the tattoos and body piercings, the drugs and bruises, Shannon can be vulnerable when she is with Lexie. When her pupils are not dilated from drugs, when her stomach is filled with hot food and she has a warm jacket, Shannon will lean back in her seat at the café, light a cigarette, and make eye contact with Lexie. It is then that she will talk about leaving the street and going straight. As she speaks, Lexie watches tenderly, knowing that to Shannon this is a dream that does not seem possible. She is saying it only to please her social worker. It is her gift, her way of saying thank you, a way to acknowledge that her well-being does matter to Lexie. Shannon is so fragile and profane that Lexie can hardly stand it at times, and she scolds herself for not toughening up. *Years of kids like her, you should know better. Nothing good is going to happen to her—stop caring. Just do your job.*

But today's meeting is different. Shannon is still high on something, anxious to go out with Lexie. When she has money, Shannon is generous, eager to be the host and to share her largesse. She buys Lexie's coffee, and orders a hamburger, fries, and milk for herself. She insists that Lexie have a donut. Later, when the food is eaten, she leans back. "I've got something to tell you. I don't know if you'll be mad or not." She pauses and smiles almost shyly. "I want you to be happy with me."

Lexie knows immediately that Shannon is pregnant. She has dreaded this day—all her talks about birth control and responsibility have never been successful. Her stomach tightens. She is appalled, although careful not to let this show on her face. But Shannon already senses Lexie's reaction. She becomes defensive, and her face shuts down as she grabs the bill and her purse in preparation for a dramatic exit.

"I'm clean," she insists. "I haven't used or had a drink since I found out. I'm even cutting back on cigarettes. Stevie's looking after me now."

"Stevie's your pimp," Lexie exclaims harshly. "How does he even know if it's his baby?" Instantly she berates herself for asking this. It will lead nowhere, except to satisfy her own curiosity about how these two lost souls will declare ownership of the baby.

"It's his alright. We're sure of it 'cause I haven't had a john for two months—since my last period. Stevie doesn't want me to put out any more." She smiles smugly at this evidence of his love.

"You'll have to start seeing a doctor regularly and eat properly. Have you looked at all your options—adoption, abortion?" But Lexie knows that Shannon will not hear a word against her keeping this baby. After all, this baby will be the first person in her life who is sure to love her. This will be her only real possession. Lexie cautions herself. *Start using your skills. Quit being emotional—you'll only lose her.*

Shannon shakes her head angrily. "I want my baby." She leans forward across the table, pointing her index finger for emphasis. "This is mine. Me and Stevie have plans. We're getting an apartment, just the two of us and later the baby, of course." She challenges Lexie. "Stevie says he wants to meet you."

Lexie nods. She understands that Stevie feels the need to put her in her place, to discredit her in front of Shannon so that his power over her is complete. She knows she has enough experience and skill to beat him at that game. "That will be fine, because I'm worrying already, Shannon. Having a baby is a wonderful thing, but it's a lifelong commitment. How will you look after it? Stevie's a pimp and a drug pusher, and I know that he's beaten you."

Remember your own childhood, you stupid, stupid girl. It was the same for your mother. As soon as you were born, her pimp put her back to work, and she worked and drugged until she died. She'd already lost you to welfare when you were seven. But she had you long enough to mess you up permanently. And now you're going to do it all over again. Lexie knows she will speak some version of this truth to Shannon in the next few weeks.

Lexie can no longer bear any more of this conversation, or the sight of Shannon. She tells her she has another appointment and asks her to call to set up a time to meet Stevie. She already knows what he'll be like. She's met lots of young pimps before, and she also knows that they come from dysfunctional families similar to Shannon's. While driving back to the office, she sees the image of Shannon on the day she was apprehended from her mother, nearly eight and a half years ago. How extremely tiny and fragile she had been then, and how readily she had come away with Lexie. She had helped Lexie gather a bag of clothes, careful to step around her stoned mother, who was sprawled on the floor against the edge of the dirty bed in their shabby motel room. It was Shannon who had phoned the police and asked them to get Lexie, her mom's social worker, because, in her own words, "We need some help, I think." Lexie's stomach hurts at the memory.

She realizes that the nausea she is experiencing, the pain in her viscera that she has experienced throughout her years of social work, is happening again because once more she has allowed herself to become attached. She suddenly remembers Helen, another social worker she knew years ago, who, upon reading a letter from a young woman she had worked with for years, simply picked up her purse and walked away, leaving clients and stunned co-workers behind forever. Lexie is tempted to do the same. *Just turn right instead of left at the next set of lights and go home.*

She knows Andy would be glad to have her there and that they'd get along all right without her salary. She could paint and read and garden, and maybe go fishing. She wheels into the government parking lot, determined. *I'll write a letter of expectation to Shannon and Stevie right now. Put it in writing—drug and alcohol counselling, prenatal classes.* She turns off the engine and pulls the key from the ignition. Shannon will have to submit to weekly blood tests to check for drugs in her system. And they'll both have to agree to co-operate completely with regular home visits by a social worker after the baby is born. She allows herself one of her mother's patented deep sighs. *Ah, hell. That baby still won't have a chance, not with Shannon and Stevie. They're just too messed up.*

She sits at her office desk staring at the blank screen of her computer, while in her mind, she riffles through the faces from years of social work, like the telephone numbers in her Rolodex. She doesn't recall all their names, but she remembers how they smiled or shouted or cried. She remembers their aggression, their vulnerability. She knows how rich she is in her collection of human experience. She can reach in her memory box and bring out the devastated face of a brave young girl giving up her baby for adoption. She can pick out

202 ❦ DEANNA LUEDER

the joyful face of the adoptive mother who has tears rolling down her cheeks as she holds the baby she thought she'd never have. Lexie can see faces of greed, hate, evil, cowardice, of liars and manipulators, of twisted perversions, of bewildered, frightened victims, and admittedly in fewer numbers, she can see faces of unselfish giving and loving, of immense quiet courage and forgiveness.

She switches on the computer, and without hesitation types the letter of expectation for Shannon and Stevie. She leaves space at the bottom, not only for her signature, but for that of her supervisor, to give the document more impact. She prints two copies and puts them aside for her supervisor to sign.

Then she types her letter of resignation. Before she prints it off, she rereads it. Lexie wishes that there were some appropriate place in it for thanking all of her clients over the past several decades. Willingly or unwillingly, they have shared intimate experiences and perspectives that have humbled her time and time again. She is grateful to them all for enriching and enlightening her, for touching and tearing her heart, and for challenging her attitudes. But most of all, they have taught her a point of view that is now forever shaded grey—infinitesimal refinements with perhaps one or two strands of unrelenting black and shining white.

AFTERWORD

MY ENTRY INTO SOCIAL WORK WAS LARGELY ACCIDENTAL. After I obtained my Bachelor of Arts degree at the University of Saskatchewan in 1965, employers from various fields came onto campus to recruit employees. Of the three jobs I was offered, social work sounded the most intriguing, though I had only a vague notion of what was involved. I never guessed that it would be my career for the next thirty years.

My first caseload in rural Saskatchewan—termed *generalized child welfare*—included everything from youth probation to adoption to child protection investigations sometimes with subsequent court work, to supervising foster homes and the children placed in them. It was a baptism in deep waters, and I could barely swim. But we new social workers formed a tight group, soul-searching on weekends as we discussed cases ad infinitum, while drinking plenty of beer and wine in one another's ratty basement suites.

As I was torturing myself about a case one day, I remember the gentle words of a wise, seasoned social worker, "You know, Deanna, you don't have to know all the answers ... but you have to ask the right questions ... and listen to the silences." After a pause, while I nodded thoughtfully, she continued, "But you must read, read, read. Books on child development, on behavioural analysis, on addiction, anything you can find."

I've gradually come to believe that the basic characteristics of a competent social worker are formed in childhood: respect, empathy, compassion, and intuition (the famous "flinch factor"). But it is education and experience that enhance and refine these skills, enabling social workers to support clients as they discover their own strengths.

I began writing these stories to invite the public into the real world of the child protection and family services social worker. My greatest concern and care was given to the depiction of the fictional characters. The main character, Lexie Doucette, is not a representation of any real social worker, except for some of her youthful experiences and the trek across Canada, which loosely follows mine. The client situations described in the stories have not been based on real cases or people with whom I have worked. However, they encapsulate daily occurrences that every frontline social worker has coped with. Indeed, many have coped with far more challenging situations than those I chose to write about.

I hope that the writing will give credence to a much-maligned profession and reveal to the reader that it is indeed a worthy one, not to be dismissed as mere "do-gooding" or as a job of unrelieved doom and gloom. Social work is a profession that is perfect for the curious learner, the optimist, the communicator, and the lover of life.